THE DESPERADO

THE DESPERADO

CLIFTON ADAMS

WHEELER PUBLISHING
A part of Gale, Cengage Learning

Detroit • New York • San Francisco • New Haven, Conn • Waterville, Maine • London

GALE
CENGAGE Learning®

LIBRARY OF CONGRESS CATALOGING-IN-PUBLICATION DATA

Adams, Clifton.
  The desperado / by Clifton Adams. — Large print ed.
    p. cm. — (Wheeler Publishing large print western)
  ISBN-13: 978-1-4104-4770-8 (pbk.)
  ISBN-10: 1-4104-4770-7 (pbk.)
  1. Large type books. I. Title.
PS3551.D34D47 2012
813'.54—dc23   2012001787

Published in 2012 by arrangement with Golden West Literary Agency.

Printed in the United States of America
1 2 3 4 5   16 15 14 13 12
FD123

THE DESPERADO

CHAPTER 1

I awoke suddenly and lay there in the darkness, listening to the rapid, faraway thud of hoofbeats. The horse was traveling fast, and occasionally the rhythmic gait would falter and become uneven, then catch and come on again in the direction of the ranch house. It was a tired horse. It had been pushed hard and for too long. I could tell by the way it was running.

Pa had heard it too. I heard the bedsprings screech downstairs as he got up. Then the old wall clock began to clang monotonously. I didn't bother to count the strokes, but I knew it must be twelve o'clock. The hoofbeats were getting louder now.

I got up and pulled on my pants. I found my boots under the bed and stuffed my feet into them without bothering to light the lamp. Then, holding onto the banister, I felt my way downstairs and into the parlor.

Pa was standing at the front door, a slight

breeze coming through the doorway and flapping the white cotton nightshirt against his bare legs. He was standing there peering into the darkness, holding a shotgun in the crook of his arm.

"Tall?" he said without looking around.

"Yes, sir."

"You better get that forty-four out of the bureau drawer. It's in there with my shirts somewhere. You can find it."

I said, "Yes, sir," and turned and felt my way into the downstairs bedroom that Pa and Ma used. Ma was sitting up in bed, her nightgown a white blob in the darkness and her nightcap a smaller blob above it. I went to the bureau and started feeling around in the drawer until I found the pistol.

"Talbert," Ma said anxiously, "what is it, son?"

"Just a rider, Ma. Nothing to worry about."

"What are you looking for there in the bureau?"

"Pa's pistol," I said. "Just in case."

She didn't say anything for a moment. But she was worried. She had been worried ever since I'd got into that scrape with the state police down at Garner's Store. But that had been a long time ago, almost six months. Anyway, I hadn't killed anybody; I'd just

8

beaten hell out of a carpetbagger with the butt end of a Winchester. There had been a big stir about it for a while, but Pa had fixed it up with the bluebelly police for fifty head of three-year-old cattle. So I wasn't worried about that.

I said, "Rest easy, Ma. It's probably one of the neighbors. Maybe somebody's sick."

She still didn't say anything, so I went back into the parlor where Pa was. We heard the horse pull up and scamper nervously, and we knew the rider was swinging open the rail gate about two hundred yards south of the house.

Pa said, "Tall?" That's the way Pa would do when he was worrying something in his mind. He'd call your name and wait for you to answer before he'd come out and say what he was thinking.

"Yes, sir," I said.

"Tall, you haven't been up to anything, have you? You haven't got into any trouble that you haven't told us about?"

"No, sir," I said.

I could feel Pa relax. Then he reached over and roughed up my hair, the way he used to do when I was just a kid, when he was feeling good. Pa could stand just about anything but a liar, and he knew I'd tell him the truth, no matter what it was.

The rider was coming on now, and we could hear the horse blowing and grunting. The rider swung down at the hitching rack by our front porch and called out:

"Mr. Cameron! Tall!"

It was Ray Novak's voice. I would have known it anywhere. He was two or three years older than me, and his pa used to be town marshal in John's City, before the scalawags and turncoats came in and elected their own man. Ray was old enough to have fought a year for the Confederacy, and that set him apart from the rest of us who had been too young. Ordinarily, he was an easygoing, likable man, and the only thing I had against him was that he had been seeing a little too much of Laurin Bannerman. But that wasn't important. I knew how Laurin felt, and I knew I didn't have anything to be afraid of on that score. From Ray Novak or anybody else.

Pa pushed the screen door open and stepped out on the front porch. "Ray?" he said. "Ray Novak?"

"Yes, sir," Ray said.

"Well, come on in," Pa said. "Tall, light the table lamp, will you? And see if the kitchen stove's still warm. Pull the coffee pot up on the front lid if it is."

I lit the lamp and went back to the kitchen.

The fire had gone out in the stove. When I came back to the parlor, Ray was saying, "I'm afraid I can't stay, Mr. Cameron. The truth is I just stopped by to see if I could change my horse for a fresh mount. That animal of mine is about played out." He saw me then and we nodded to each other.

Ray Novak didn't look scared exactly, but he looked worried. He took off his hat and ran his fingers through thick, straw-colored hair. "I played the fool down in John's City this afternoon," he said. "I let myself get suckered into a scrape with the police. I guess I'll have to get out of the country for a while, until things cool off a little."

Pa looked at him sharply. "You . . . didn't kill anybody, did you, Ray?"

Killing a state policeman in Texas, in 1869, was the same as buying a one-way ticket to a hanging. The bluebellies from the North had their own judges and juries, and their verdict was always the same.

But Ray shook his head. "It was just a fist fight," he said. "But they're pretty riled up. I was in the harness shop getting a splice made in a stirrup strap and this private cavalryman came in and started passing remarks about all the families around John's City — all the families that amounted to anything before the war. When he started

11

on 'that goddamn Novak white trash that used to be town marshal,' I hit him. I busted a couple of teeth, I think. I expect a detachment of cavalry will be along pretty soon, looking for me. I don't aim to be around."

Pa nodded soberly. "It was a damn fool thing to do all right," he said. "And you won't be able to fix it with the police this time. First Tall, and now you. The Yankees'll feel bound to do something about it this time."

Ray looked down at his feet and shifted uncomfortably. "Yes, sir," he said. "That's about the way I figured it. That's one reason I came by your place. If they don't find me they might get to remembering Tall and start on him again." Then he looked up at me, his big bland face as serious as a preacher's. "I'm sorry, Tall, I didn't figure to get you mixed up in it."

"What the hell," I said. "The only thing I'm sorry about is that you didn't put a bullet in the bluebelly's gut."

"Tall?" Pa said.

"Yes, sir."

"Now just hold your head. Ray's right. This could be serious for both of you. We better take a little time and figure something out. Ray, have you figured on anything?"

"I thought maybe I'd go up to the Panhandle for a while, sir. I've got an older brother up there that has a little spread. I could work with him through the spring gathering season and come back in the summer. That ought to be time enough to let it blow over."

Pa thought about it, standing there in his nightshirt, still holding that shotgun in the crook of his arm. "Maybe," he said. "But the Panhandle isn't far enough. Tall's got an uncle down on the Brazos. You boys could stay there. I could write you a letter when it looks all right to come back."

Maybe I was still half asleep. Anyway, it was just coming to me what they were talking about. I said, "Just a minute, Pa. I don't aim to run. This isn't my scrape, it's Ray's."

"Tall?"

"Yes, sir," I said from force of habit.

"Now listen to me," Pa said soberly. "Pretty soon they'll be coming. When they don't find Ray they're going to be mad, and it won't take them long to remember that carpetbagger you clubbed with a rifle stock. You know what kind of a chance you'll have if the scalawags decide to bring it to court."

For a minute I didn't say anything. I knew Pa was right. If they didn't find Ray, they would be coming for me. The smart thing to do would be to get out of the country for

13

a while. But knowing it didn't make me like it.

I liked things just the way they were. I liked it here on the ranch — being able to ride over to the Bannerman spread every day or so to see Laurin, going into John's City once a month when they held the dances in Community Hall. I liked it just fine right where I was, and I hated the idea of being chased away by a bunch of damned Yankee bluebellies and blacks who had been slaves only a few years ago. And pretty soon some of that hate began to direct itself at Ray Novak.

I looked at Ray and he knew how I was beginning to feel about it. He was sorry. But a hell of a lot of good that was going to do. He stood there shifting from one foot to the other, uncomfortably. He was a big man, and he couldn't have been more than twenty-one years old. But that didn't make him young. In this country a boy started being a man as soon as he could strap on a gun. And about the first thing a boy did, after he learned to walk and ride, was to strap on a gun.

Before I could say what I was thinking, before Ray Novak could put his discomfort into words, Ma came out of the bedroom and stood looking at us with worried eyes.

Ma was a thin, work-weary woman, not really old, but looking old. There were deep lines around her pale eyes that came from worry and trying to gouge a living from this wild land. Ma had been pretty as a girl. There were faded pictures of her in an old album that gave you an idea how she must have looked when she married Pa. The pictures showed a young girl dressed in the rather daring fashion of the day — those low-cut dresses that all the great ladies of the Confederacy used to wear with such a casual air, as they sat queenlike, smiling and pouring tea from silver pots into delicate china cups. It was hard to believe that Ma had been one of those great ladies once. Her father had been a rich tobacco buyer in Virginia, but he lost everything in the war and died soon afterward.

I never saw Virginia myself. And those pictures in the album were just pictures to me, but I guess Pa still saw her as she had looked then, because something happened to him every time he looked at her. His wind-reddened face softened and his stern eyes became gentle — even as they did now as he saw her standing in the doorway.

She stood there, holding her cotton wrap-around together, smiling quickly at Ray.

"Good evening, Ray," she said.

15

"Good evening, Mrs. Cameron," Ray said uneasily.

"Mother," Pa said, "why don't you go back to bed? I'll be along in a few minutes."

But she shook her head. "I want to know what it's about. Tell me, Rodger, because I'll find out sooner or later."

"It's nothing serious," Pa said gently. "Ray just had some trouble in John's City with the state police. It's nothing to worry about."

"I don't understand," Ma said vaguely. "What has that to do with Talbert?"

"I just think it's best if they both go away for a while, until it blows over. There's been no killing. Just a fist fight. But there's no telling what the Yankee troopers will do while they're riled up. I'll send Ray and Tall down to my brother's place on the Brazos. You know how the police shift from one place to another. In a few months there won't be anybody around John's City to remember or hold a grudge, and then they can come back."

She considered it carefully, but I knew she wouldn't question Pa's word. That's the way it always had been.

"All right, Rodger," she said at last. "Whatever you say."

Her voice was heavy and edged with

16

hopelessness. She had had great plans for me. Even before I was born she had started making plans to send me to the University of Virginia and make a lawyer out of me, or maybe a preacher. But the war had put an end to that. There wasn't anybody in Texas, except the scalawags and bureau agents, that had money enough to send their children off to places like Virginia. And I hadn't made things any easier for Ma. I had come into the world in the midst of great pain, almost killing her, and I had been a source of pain ever since. Like the time I cut Criss Bagley open with a pocketknife. She had tried to comfort me and to understand, and I had tried to explain to her. But I couldn't explain when I didn't know myself. I just knew that Criss had been coming at me with an elm club and I knew I had to get it away from him, one way or another. Criss was twelve and I was ten, and he outweighed me by thirty pounds or more, so the knife seemed the only way.

I remember the way he looked, standing there with his eyes wide in amazement — before the pain — staring down at his opened belly. We had been swimming down at Double-dare Hole, a muddy, deep hole in the arroyo that cut across our land, and in the spring and early summer it was almost always full. It was June, I remember, and four of us had stopped there on our way from school. And one of the kids — I don't know which one — tied knots in Criss's clothes, and that was the way it started. He thought I did it. He came out of the water yelling, "Goddamn you, Tall Cameron!" And I remember saying, "Don't goddamn me! I didn't tie knots in your dirty damn clothes!"

For a while we just stood there glaring at each other. Criss was naked and dripping, and fat around the belly and hips, like a girl, I had already dried myself in the sun and had my clothes on. The other two boys climbed up on the bank, grinning. Then one of them said, "What's the matter, Criss? You afraid of Tall? You just goin' to stand there and let him get away with tyin' knots in your clothes?"

Criss turned on the boy. "Keep your goddamn mouth shut. I guess I know how to take care of Tall Cameron . . . unless he wants to untie my clothes, that is."

I know now that Criss really didn't want to fight. But I didn't know it then. I could have untied his clothes and that would have been the end of it. Instead, I said, "You can untie them yourself if you want them untied. I don't guess I'm bound to wait on you."

Criss was one of those people who never tanned in the summer, no matter how much he stayed out in the sun. His hair was kind of a dirty yellow, and so were his eyebrows; and his skin was as pink and soft as a baby's bottom. He stood there waiting for me to do something about his clothes. His pale little eyes shut down to angry slits.

"I'll count to ten," he said tightly. "If you don't have my clothes untied by then, it's goin' be too bad."

"You can count to ten thousand," I said. "I told you I didn't do it."

So he started counting. And I didn't move. And when he had finished he said, "All right, goddamn you!" and started toward me.

I had never fought Criss before. I'd never wanted to because of his size, but I wasn't afraid of him. And, after the first swing he took, I saw that it was going to be easy. He was big and fat and clumsy, and not very smart. I ducked under his fist and slammed him right in the middle of his pink, fat belly. He eyes flew open in surprise and he made a sound like a horse breaking wind. I hit him again in the face, and once more in the belly, and he sat down. He didn't fall or stumble. He just sat down. And when he got up again he had that stick in his hand.

I don't even remember getting the knife out of my pocket. I just remember Criss flailing away with that club, catching me once on the left shoulder and numbing it. Then he came in to hit me again, and that was when I cut him. Right across the belly. You could see layers of fat meat as the gash began to open. And at first little droplets of bright blood appeared like sweat on the raw edges of the cut. Then Criss sat down again, very carefully, and then he lay down and began to cry.

"Goddamn you, Tall! You killed me!"

For a minute I thought maybe I had. The blood was coming faster now, oozing out of the white gash and over his pink skin. I still wasn't scared, but I knew I'd have to get out of John's City if he died, and I would have to do it before the town marshal heard about it. That was when Ray Novak's pa was marshal, old Martin Novak, and he had a reputation for tracking killers. So I left Criss where he was, there on the ground, crying, and ran all the way to our ranch house.

I told Pa what had happened, and I remember him staring at me for a long, long time and not saying anything. He grew to be an old man in those few minutes. And he had been an old man ever since. At last he said, "Tall?"

"Yes, sir."

"You go to the house. You go to your room and stay there. Don't tell your ma anything about it until I get back. Give me your word."

I had to give him my word. And I had to stay with it, because that's the way it was between me and Pa. I went to the house, and from my room I watched Pa get the spring wagon hitched and head down toward the arroyo.

Criss didn't die, but there were some anxious days. Old man Bagley swore that he would kill me, and Pa too, if Criss died. But he didn't die. He stayed in bed for about two months and then he got up as well as anybody, except for an eight-inch scar across his belly, just below the navel.

I tried to explain to Ma the way it happened — the way Criss had come at me with that stick — but it wasn't any use. She would always end up by crying, "But son, why didn't you run from him? Why didn't you untie his clothes for him?" And I couldn't tell her. I didn't know myself.

So, for some reason, that was what I thought about as Ma stood there in the doorway holding her wrap-around together, and looking at Pa, and me, and Ray Novak.

As she said:

"All right, Rodger. Whatever you say."

I said, "It's going to be all right, Ma. We'll just put in the spring working, and come home in the summer."

For a moment I forgot that I didn't want to leave the John's City country, that I didn't want to go away from Laurin, that I was mad at Ray Novak for bringing all this on. I wanted to see Ma smile more than anything else.

And she did, finally, but it was weak, not reaching her eyes. She said, "Of course, son. Will you be going . . . right away?"

I looked at Pa and he nodded. "Yes," he said. "Right away."

Ma went into the kitchen and we heard her shaking the grate on the cookstove. Pa said, "Ray, did you come by your pa's place?"

"No, sir," Ray said. "I figured that would be the first place the posse would look for me."

Pa nodded soberly. "You did right. I'll go over and let him know that you're all right. I'll do it tomorrow."

"I'd be much obliged, sir."

Pa went into the bedroom and put on his pants and boots. He came out stuffing his nightshirt in his pants. Without saying anything, he handed me a cartridge belt with an open holster attached to it. I buckled the belt on and he slid the .44 into the holster, then I went upstairs to change my own nightshirt for a regular shirt and a mackinaw.

The whole thing struck me as something out of a dream. Only a few minutes ago I had been sound asleep, with not a worry in the world, unless maybe it was figuring out a way to see Laurin more often. And now I was getting ready to leave. Going down on the Brazos to a strange country that I had never seen before. Just because Ray Novak lost his fool head and hit a Yankee cavalryman.

I heard the front door open and close, and there was a thud of boots and a bright sound of spurs as Pa and Ray went out to the barn to get the horses ready. There was a familiar stirring sound downstairs, wooden spoon against crock bowl, and I knew Ma was mixing a batter of some kind. Ma was like most women. In case of death or any other disaster, her first thought was of food. The women themselves never eat the food, but cooking gives them something to do. It takes their minds off their troubles. Maybe it's the same as a man getting drunk to forget his troubles. A woman cooks. Anyway,

23

I knew Ray and I wouldn't go hungry on our trip to the Brazos.

I went downstairs and outside, and the night was as clean and sharp as a new knife. I stood out there for a few minutes, in the yard, looking to the west where the Bannerman spread was. I thought about Laurin. I let myself wonder if Laurin would miss me. If she would miss Ray Novak — even a little bit. Goddamn Ray Novak, anyway.

Pa and Ray were working quietly in the barn, in the sickly orange light of an oil lantern. Pa had cut out two horses from the holding corral, and I saw immediately that one of them was the big copper-colored gelding that was registered in the horse book as Red Hawk. But he was just "Red" to me, and beautiful as only a pure-bred Morgan can be. Ray was throwing a saddle up on a sturdy little black and Pa was taking care of Red, patting him gently and crooning into his nervous pointed little ears.

I came up and slapped Red on his smooth glossy rump and he switched his fine head around and glared at me with a caustic eye. Red was bigger than most Morgans, almost sixteen hands high and king every inch of the way. The extra height was mostly in his hard-muscled legs, which gave him speed. A barrel chest and a heart as big as Texas gave him the stamina to do a hard day's work and not complain, although he had been bred as a show horse. An Eastern pilgrim had brought him down from Vermont or Massachusetts or somewhere two summers ago when the horse had been a two-year-old, and it had been love at first sight between Red and Pa. Pa had bought him on the spot, and Ma and me still didn't know what Red cost.

Pa looked up at me as he tightened the cinch under Red's belly. "I guess Red will get you to Brazos country," he said, "and get you back again."

I didn't know what to say. I knew how Pa felt about that blueblood, and there were other horses on the place that would do just as well for me. But I found the good sense to keep my mouth shut. Pa was giving Red to me and he wanted to do it his own way.

After a while, Ma came out with some things for me done up in a blanket roll, and she had a grub sack filled with coffee and bacon and meal and salt and some fresh-cooked cornbread. And there was a small deep skillet done up in the blanket roll. I couldn't help grinning a little. It was more like getting ready for a picnic or a camp meeting than making a cross-country run with a posse on our tails.

I said, "Thanks, Ma. Now don't you worry." Then I kissed her cheek, and her skin was dry and rough against my lips. Her eyes were wide — a little too wide, and liquid-looking, but not a tear spilled out. She would wait until I was gone for that. I swung up on Red and Pa handed up a sealed white envelope.

"This is for your Uncle George Cameron," he said quietly. "Give it to him when you get to the ranch. It tells him who you are and asks him to give both of you a job of work through the spring season. It doesn't say anything about the police trouble. I don't figure there's any use worrying him about that."

He stopped and raked his fingers through his thinning hair. Pa had been a handsome man not many years before, and part of that handsomeness could still be seen. Men hold up better than women in this country. But he looked tired and old as he reached up to shake hands with me. Most of the age was in his eyes.

"Good-by, Tall. Be careful of yourself."

"Sure, Pa."

"Do you think you can find the place all right?"

"We can't miss the Brazos if we ride east," I said. "We'll head south and then ask questions if we have to."

He nodded. "I guess that's about right. Good-by, Ray. I'll let your pa know."

"Good-by, sir. Thank you."

We sat there for a minute, wondering if there was anything else to say. Then we all began to hear the noise of complex rattle and movement. For an instant I listened and looked at Ray Novak. He was thinking the same as I was. There was a rattle of loose steel and the aching screech of saddle leather, all muted and deadened by night and the distance. Then came the thudding of regimented horses, and we didn't have to be told that they were cavalry horses.

And still we sat there as the sound of horses and the rattle of cavalry sabers got closer. And I thought grimly, They sure as hell didn't waste time! Then I raked Red with the blunted rowels of my spurs, and we jumped out of the barn and into the darkness, with Ray Novak right behind.

The detachment of troopers saw us, or heard us. Somebody, an officer probably, bellowed out, "Halt! In the name of the United States Army!"

I sank the steel into Red and we jumped out a full length in front of Ray and the black. The cavalry recovered quickly and there were more bellowed orders in the darkness. Then they were coming after us, at full charge, from the way it sounded.

CHAPTER 2

It's fine to feel a horse like Red under you. I bent over his neck and felt the long hard muscles along his shoulders as he began to stretch out in a long, flowing, ground-eating stride. Then the cavalry started shooting, but that didn't worry me much. They couldn't hit anything in the darkness unless somebody got pretty lucky. And Ray and I had one advantage over them. We knew the country.

We headed south first, toward some low rolling hills where the mesquite and scrub oak was so thick that it was hard to get through, even in the daytime, if you didn't know your way around. Red was running like a well-oiled machine now, and Ray's black horse was about two jumps behind us. The black was a good horse, but he was used mostly for cutting cattle and I knew he wouldn't hold up at the pace we were going for more than a half a mile. So I turned in the saddle and yelled back at Ray Novak.

"We'll head for the arroyo and take Daggert's Road!"

Ray yelled something, but the wind snatched the words away before they got to me. Anyway, I figured he understood. It was the natural thing to do if you knew the country, and Ray knew it as well as I did. We went barreling across the flatland, pulling away from the cavalry a little, but not enough to get lost. And then we blasted into the hills, into the dagger-thorned chaparral and clawlike scrub oaks that grew as thick as weeds. In the pale moonlight, we were able to look for familiar trails and find them, but I hated to think what Red's glossy coat was going to look like when we came out of it.

The cavalry made up some lost time as we thrashed our way through the brush. They were coming into shooting range again, they had their carbines out now, pumping lead in our general direction, and I began to be afraid that somebody was going to get lucky after all if they kept that up for long.

But we blasted our way through the brush and went barreling down the slope again toward the ugly dark gash in the land below us, the arroyo. The spring rains hadn't come yet, so the sandy weed-grown bed was still dry as we slid our horses down the steep bank. The shooting had stopped again. I figured the cavalry had hit the brush and was having its hands full there. So we pounded on down the dry wash and finally we came to what we were looking for, a cutaway in the bank of the wash, only you had to know where it was to see it, especially at night. It was grown over with weeds and scrub trees, and it stayed that way the year around except for maybe two months in the spring when the rains up north set the wash to flowing.

That was Daggert's Road. If you knew where to look, there was room enough to squeeze a horse through the opening, through the hanging vines and scrubs, and you entered into a kind of a trail that wound up into the hill country. If you followed the trail far enough you'd find a little lean-to shack against a hillside, falling to pieces and rotten with years. Old-timers would tell you that shack used to be Sam Daggert's head-quarters, that he used to hide out there after making one of his raids on the wagon trains crossing the Santa Fe Trail.

I don't know about the Sam Daggert part, but I know the cabin is there, and somebody must have made that trail for some reason.

I used to ride out this way with Pa some-times, looking for strays. And, kidlike, I would poke around the shack looking for buried treasure, or maybe skeletons or guns. But all I ever found was a few soggy, black-ened bits of paper that might have been paper cartridges at one time.

Well, Sam Daggert or not, whoever made the trail, I was grateful to him. Ray Novak was first to go through the opening because his black was smaller than Red. Then I shoved Red through, and took a minute to rearrange the vines. We could hear the cavalry just beginning to jump their horses down the bank of the wash.

We waited where we were until they pounded past us, running south in the bend of the arroyo. And for a minute there I felt pretty good about it. I was pretty pleased with myself. I wasn't scared, for one thing, and hadn't been, through the whole busi-ness. And I don't think it had entered my mind that the cavalry would catch us, and even if they had caught us, they couldn't have done anything.

It wasn't cockiness exactly. It was train-ing. One Texan was better than a whole god-damned regiment of bluebelly Yankees. I was as sure of that as I was sure the sun would come up the next morning. The War between the States hadn't changed that. So that was the way I thought. Only it wasn't thinking, it was knowing, and for a few minutes there I didn't hate Ray Novak for getting me into this mess, because I was enjoying myself.

But not Ray. His face was whiter than the pale moonlight that sifted through the brush. He wiped his face on his shirt sleeve and looked at me and Red, and then at his own black horse, as if he was surprised to see that we were still in one piece.

He said finally, "I guess I didn't bargain for a thing like this."

"For a thing like what?"

"I didn't figure they'd be so worked up. You'd think I'd killed somebody, from the way they came after us."

I couldn't figure Ray Novak out. He acted scared, but I knew he wasn't — or at least I'd never known him to be scared of anything before. He sat there, looking at me with those sober eyes of his, and wiping his face. "I don't like it at all."

"For God's sake," I said, "what don't you like about it? We got away from them, didn't we?"

He didn't say anything, so I pulled Red around and nudged him forward, heading north. I could almost feel Ray stiffen in surprise.

"Now where are you going? I had an idea we were headed east."

I said, "We're going away, aren't we? That's the time for saying good-by, isn't it?"

He knew I was headed for the Bannerman spread to see Laurin before starting the long ride to the Brazos. I half expected him to go on without me. At least, I expected an argument of some kind, but strangely enough he didn't offer any. He reined the black over and fell in beside me.

The Bannerman ranch house was dark when we got there, but it wasn't long before we saw somebody light a lamp and come out on the front porch. It was Joe Bannerman, Laurin's brother, holding a big hogleg six-shooter in one hand and the lamp in the other.

Before he decided to shoot first and ask questions later, I called, "It's me, Joe — Tall Cameron. Ray Novak's here with me."

I heard him grunt in surprise as Ray and I swung around the hitching rack in the front yard, making for the back of the house.

I said, "Blow the lamp out, Joe. The cavalry's after us. I don't think they're anywhere close, but there's no use taking chances."

"What the hell have you got yourself into

now?" he said. He sounded half mad at being jarred out of bed at that time of night. But the lamp went out and he padded barefoot to the end of the porch, peering at us through the darkness. "Ray Novak, is that you?" Then we heard him spit in the darkness. "Has this young heller got you mixed up in some of his shenanigans?"

Joe never liked me much. He was a lot older than Laurin, and I knew he never liked it much when I came calling. But to hell with Joe Bannerman. Laurin was the one I'd come to say good-by to.

"It's me, all right, Joe," Ray Novak said, "but the trouble we're in is my fault. Tall didn't have anything to do with it."

For a moment, Joe didn't say anything. Then, "Well, I'll be damned. . . ."

Ray started explaining about his fight with the bluebelly back in John's City, but I didn't stay to hear about it. Just then I saw her standing there at the back door. I dropped down from the saddle and gave Red a slap on the rump, sending him on around to the back of the house.

"Tall?"

She looked like a pale ghost, or an angel, standing there in the darkness. Her voice was anxious, touched with fear. Then she pushed the screen door open and came

35

outside. She stood there on the top step, covered in one of those pale, shapeless wrap-arounds that all women seem to reach for when they get out of bed. I had never seen her like that before. In the pale moonlight, her face seemed even more beautiful than I had remembered it, and her dark hair was unbraided, falling around her shoulders as soft as a dark mist. I stood there at the bottom of the steps, looking up at her.

"Tall," she said urgently, "something's wrong. You wouldn't be here at this time of night unless . . ."

"It's nothing," I said. "We're going down on the Brazos for a spell. I wanted to say good-by, that's all."

"We?" I don't think she had known there were two of us until then.

"Me and Ray Novak," I said. "He took a swing at a bluebelly and got the cavalry on him. Now they're after both of us."

She made a startled little sound, and I wanted to reach up and put my arms around her and tell her not to worry. I'd be back. All the bluebellys north of the Rio Grande couldn't keep me away from her.

But I didn't move. Joe Bannerman would have shot me in a minute if he had caught me laying a hand on his sister while she was still in her nightclothes. And probably that was just what Joe was expecting. He moved around to the corner of the house, still talking to Ray Novak, but careful not to let me out of his sight.

She lowered her voice, but the worry and urgency were still there. "Tall, are you sure . . . are you sure that you haven't . . . done anything?"

That would have made me mad if it had been anybody else. Nobody seemed to believe me when I told them that Ray Novak was the one that started all the trouble. They seemed to think that Ray Novak was incapable of getting into any trouble, especially on the wrong side of the law. With Tall Cameron, that was the thing they expected.

But I couldn't get mad at Laurin. I said, "Don't worry about me. We'll put in a spell on the Brazos, until things settle down, and then I'll be coming back. Don't forget that. I'll be back."

At last she seemed to believe me. She smiled faintly and started to come down the steps, but a sullen grunt from her brother stopped her.

Damn Joe Bannerman, anyway. And Ray Novak. This was a hell of a way for a man to say good-by to his best girl. His only girl. I heard a rustling around inside the house, and then a match flared and lighted a lamp-wick. That would be Old Man Bannerman coming out to see what the fuss was about, and I didn't feel like I wanted to go through the whole rigmarole again, explaining that we were in trouble and it was Ray who started it and not me.

Ray Novak called, "We'd better be riding, Tall."

I knew he was right. There was no sense in staying here and letting the bluebellies finally stumble on us.

I was standing there, feeling helpless. One moment Laurin's face was quiet and composed, and the next moment it began to break up around her eyes. Then, somehow, she was in my arms.

"Laurin!" Joe Bannerman roared. "For God's sake, haven't you got any decency?"

The moment was over almost before I knew she was there. But I felt better. I had held her in my arms for that short moment, and that was something they couldn't take away from me. It was something I could remember for the month, or six months, or whatever length of time we had to be apart.

She had jumped back, startled at her brother's bellowing. Then the back door opened again and the old man came out, and the lamplight splashed around until it seemed to me that the cavalry couldn't miss seeing it, no matter where they were. I knew it was time to start riding.

I got Red and led him around to the corner of the house. Ray Novak was already in the saddle, waiting for me. So I swung up, too.

Laurin's face was cameo-soft and pale in the lamplight, and that was the way I remembered it.

"Take care of yourself, Tall. Don't . . . let anything happen."

"Don't worry. There's nothing to worry about."

"Will I hear from you?"

"Sure. Anyway, I'll be back before you know it."

Ray Novak was sitting his horse impassively. Nothing showed on his face, but I could guess at what was happening inside him. All the time we had been here, Laurin hadn't even looked at him. Only when we reined our horses around to leave did she say:

"Good-by, Ray."

And he said, "Good-by, Laurin." And we rode out of the yard. I looked back once and she was still standing there by the steps, pale and beautiful in the flickering light from the oil lamp, and I realized what a lucky guy I really was. I could even afford to feel sorry for Ray Novak.

We rode east for what must have been two hours. I figured the Yankees would be so lost by now that they would be lucky to find their way home. And, as we put distance between us and John's City, I did some thinking about Ray Novak, trying to figure out what had got into him back there at Daggert's Road.

I added together all the things I knew about him and was a little surprised when it didn't come to much. The Novak ranch had been next to ours for as long as I could remember, and I had known him all that time, or thought I had known him. We had gone to Professor Bigloe's Academy together — a hell of a fancy name, I thought, for a school that held classes three times a week in the smelly parlor of Ma Simpson's boarding house, but it was the only school anywhere near John's City, and it was considered quite the thing. They said Old Man Bigloe had been a professor at the University of Virginia before they kicked him out for drunkenness. He always kept a bottle in the inside breast pocket of his frock coat, and he couldn't get through a spelling lesson without stepping back to Ma Simpson's kitchen three or four times to take a nip. Maybe he had had a good brain once, but it was fuzzy and booze-soaked by the time he opened the academy.

Anyway, he managed to get most of us through four steps of arithmetic and some spelling and history. The history and geography came together in the same class and it was the only class that Old Man Bigloe really liked. He would get to talking about Italy, and then Rome, and finally he'd get down to Caesar and he wouldn't give a damn if you threw spit balls or not. He was a thin man with a perpetual stoop to his shoulders, and sometimes he would go for two weeks without shaving. He always got a funny look in his eyes when he got to talking about Rome and those places, and it was generally agreed that he was crazy. During classes, Ma Simpson would always sit, fat and watchful, in one corner of the parlor, peeling potatoes or paring apples. She always arranged to have a murderous-looking butcher knife in her hands, just in case Old Man Bigloe had a "spell" and tried to kill somebody. But he never did.

So that was Professor Bigloe's Academy. Professor Bigloe's Academy for Learning and Culture, if you want the whole name. We went there three times a week, Mondays,

Wednesdays, and Fridays, the boys riding in on horseback. There was a lot of hell raised, and a lot of fights; but now that I came to think of it, Ray Novak hadn't figured in any of them.

Maybe it was because of his size. He was a year or two older than most of us, and big for his age anyway. But then Criss Bagley had been bigger than any of us, and that hadn't kept him out of fights. I thought about that and finally had to admit that there was something about Ray Novak — but I didn't know what — that made you think twice before starting anything with him. He always had that quiet, sober look, even as a kid, and he didn't go in much for horseplay, as most of us did. He came to Old Man Bigloe's academy for a curious reason, it seemed to the rest of us. To learn.

And, too, Ray's pa was the town marshal, and that made him something a little different. His pa had taught him everything there was to know about guns and shooting, and he was the only boy around John's City who could throw a tin can in the air and put two .44 bullets through it before it hit the ground. I only saw him do it once, but he did it so easily and perfectly that I knew it was no accident.

I don't think I ever liked Ray Novak much

after that, although I had never thought about it until now. I remember practicing with Pa's old .44, the one I was wearing now, until my thumb was raw from pulling the hammer back, but one bullet in the can was the best I could do. I think that hit me harder than anything. I didn't mind it much when Ray would make one of his occasional rides over to the Bannerman ranch — trying to act as if he was just out looking for strays, and just happened to be on that part of the range. I knew that Laurin Bannerman was the real reason for his drifting off the home range. But I also knew that he was too bashful to do anything about it, except gawk. And, anyway, Laurin was mine.

Which was fine, but it didn't tell me the reason for that scared look on Ray Novak's face back there at the arroyo, while the cavalry was pounding by.

The sky in the east began to pale and we pulled our horses up to let them blow. Ray dropped down from his saddle and stretched, and I did the same. The morning was cool, and sharp with the early-spring smell of green things. I began to think of bacon, and coffee, and fresh-cooked corn-bread.

"I figure we've got about another hour of riding time," Ray said. "We'll have to start looking for a place to bed down before long."

I said, "We'll ride until we find a place."

But Ray shook his head in that sober, solemn way of his. "I don't want to run into any more cavalry or police. Not in the daylight. We're in enough trouble as it is."

I asked a question then, one I had been remembering about: "Are you afraid of trouble?"

He looked at me and answered in one word: "Yes."

Then, after thinking a moment, he went on, "I don't like this running. If we run into the state police and they recognize us there'll be a fight, and almost always when there's a fight, somebody doesn't walk away from it. That's the kind of trouble I'm afraid of. We're on the wrong side of the law."

"What law?" I said. "The Davis police? The Yankee soldiers, and the carpetbaggers, and scalawags, and bureau agents? If that's the law, I'm just as glad to be on the other side."

But he kept shaking his head. "There has to be law."

He was a nut on the subject. The law was all he knew, I guess. He had lived it, talked it, breathed it, ever since he was old enough to know what a sheriff's star was. And he couldn't remember the time when his pa hadn't worn a star. Which was all right, as far as I was concerned — I'd never heard anything against Marshal Martin Novak. But all this talk of Reconstruction Law, as the turncoats called it, was beginning to disgust me.

I said, "Look, if you're so goddamned set on law and order, what are you running for? After you hit that cavalryman why didn't you go right on down to the jail and give yourself up? You seem to be forgetting one thing: Right now I'd be back on the ranch in my own bed if it hadn't been for you. If you hadn't come running like a wall-eyed coot and got me mixed up in it. Why did you run in the first place, that's what I want to know, if you're so damned set on the law being enforced?"

The more I talked the madder I got, and I said things that I wouldn't have said if I hadn't been so hot. It was as much my fault as his. If I hadn't clubbed that carpetbagger the Yankees wouldn't have been so worked up. Ray would have got off with a few days in jail and that would have been the end of it. But now it meant six months on the work gang, if they caught him. And me too. And I didn't intend to spend six months on the work gang, no matter whose fault it was.

For a long minute Ray Novak said nothing. In the first pale light of dawn, I could see his face getting hot and red, and I knew the smart thing to do would be to let him alone. But I was wound up and my mouth was running ahead of my thinking.

"Well," I said, "what are you going to do about it?"

He just stood there, getting hotter, and doing nothing. I guess Ray Novak wasn't used to being talked to like that. He was a lot like his pa — the quiet, serious kind, commanding respect but not making a show of it. He didn't know what to do now, with an eighteen-year-old standing up and the same as calling him yellow. For a minute I thought he might go for his gun, and at that point I didn't care one way or another.

He took a deep breath and let it out slowly, and I could almost see him taking hold of himself. He said softly, "I guess we both need some sleep. We'd better be riding on."

"Just a minute," I said. "I want to know what you're going to do. You'd better know now that if we run into any law I'm not giving myself up for a spell on the work gang. If you don't feel the same way about it, we'd better split up here and now."

He gave it careful thought before answering. "Tall," he said finally, "I told you once I was sorry for dragging you into this. That's all I can do. If I had been smart, I would have given myself up in John's City. But I wasn't smart. Now it looks like we'll have to hide out for a little while. I'll hide out but I don't intend to fight the law, if it comes to that. If you don't want to ride with me, we'll split up, and no hard feelings."

He was a hard guy to hate for a long stretch of time. He was so dead serious about everything. "Oh, hell," I said. "Let's go."

So we rode on, neither of us saying anything. For a while I amused myself by thinking of the cavalry, and how foolish they must look pounding up and down the arroyo and wondering what had happened to us. I enjoyed that. It was the same as a military victory, for the war was not over in Texas. It would never be over as long as Sheridan sent men like Throckmorton and his blue-belly generals to rule Texas with soldiers. Or men like Pease, who threw out all the judges and sheriffs and mayors who might have been able to keep some semblance of law and order and put in his own scalawags who didn't give a damn for anything except to bleed the ranchers and farmers and cotton growers, and fatten their own bank accounts back in New York or Ohio or Pennsylvania or wherever they came from. And even worse, men like E. J. Davis.

E. J. Davis, the "reconstruction governor." Colonel Davis, commanding officer of the First Texas Cavalry, U.S. Volunteers. But I'd heard him called other things, standing under the wooden awning of Garner's Store, listening to old men talk. Old men with angry faces and outraged eyes, some of them with Minie balls of the war still lodged in their lank, hungry bodies. "That bastard, Davis," was the way they usually put it. "Commanding officer of the First Texas Traitors, Cowards, and Sonsofbitches." Around the time war broke out, Davis rounded up all the scum in Texas — or that's the way I always heard it, anyway — called them the First Texas Cavalry, and offered its services to the North. And, as reward for this thoughtfulness and foresight, Sheridan, in his fine office in New Orleans, from behind a blue cloud of fifty-cent-cigar smoke, had decided that E. J. Davis was just the man for the governor's office in Texas.

Oh, there was an election. General Philip Sheridan was a man to do things right. When the people of Texas began to get restless and complained that their livestock was all dying and the children weren't getting enough to eat because the Northern army was taking everything, the General began to give it some thought. By God, if the people of Texas didn't like the army, then he would give them a governor. There would be an election and they could choose anybody they wanted.

The only trouble was, if you wanted to vote, you had to take the "Ironclad Oath," and that weeded everybody out except the newly freed slaves, and some white trash, and maybe the veterans of the First Texas Cavalry, U.S. Volunteers. Davis won in a walk. "The people's choice!" the scalawag newspapers said.

While the war was going on, I wasn't old enough to understand everything about it. But I understood the bitterness as the ranchers' big herds dwindled down to a few mangy-looking old mossyhorns, and I remembered trying to eat meat without salt because ships couldn't get through the Northern blockade. And, somehow, I knew it was all the Yankees' fault.

Hating came as natural as breathing, in those days, in Texas. I remember overhearing a conversation in front of the hardware store in John's City, where some men were laughing over the old joke of "You know what I just heard? A feller back there claims 'damn Yankee' is two words instead of one!" I laughed, but it wasn't until a couple of years later that I found out what it was about. Even Professor Bigloe said "damn-yankee" and I figured he ought to know.

That was Texas, after the war. Broke and hungry, and if it tried to lift itself to its knees it got a kick in the gut for its trouble. Pa got off easier than most ranchers, because he had been too old to go to war and was able to stay on the ranch and look after his herd. Most of the ranchers weren't so lucky. After they got back, they found that their cattle had scattered from hell to Georgia — what was left of them after the Union soldiers took what they wanted. And the Confederate soldiers too, for that matter. And the calves were unbranded and wild and belonged legally to anybody who could catch them and burn them with his own iron. Most of the cattlemen had to start all over again, and if they got their beef back it was usually with a gun. The best guarantee of ownership was a fast draw and a sure aim.

After Davis came the Davis police, or state police, and the governor was burned in effigy so often that the smell of smoke would automatically bring out a squad of soldiers with bayoneted rifles. The police were supposed to take the place of the soldiers who were being gradually drawn out of the South. But they weren't any better. They were worse, if anything.

Thinking of the Davis police brought me back to Ray Novak. Old Martin Novak was hit hardest of all by the police, because he had to sit back and watch white trash and hired gunmen take over his marshal's job and run it to suit themselves. There was no law in John's City, if you wanted to side in with the turncoats. And if you didn't, there was a law against everything. A rancher could be fined a hundred dollars for elbowing his way to a saloon bar, and, if he didn't have the money to pay, it would be taken out in beef cattle, with a dozen or so of the police going along to see that the collection was made. And all Martin Novak could do was watch. And wait. And hope that someday things would change and he could bring another kind of law back to John's City.

And Ray . . . Maybe that was what he was afraid of — of hurting his pa's chances of getting back into office. Maybe that was the reason he was so anxious to avoid any kind of brush with the law.

I was tired thinking about it. Maybe he was just plain yellow and had a streak up his back that you couldn't cover with both hands. I decided that when we started riding the next night Ray could go his way and I'd go mine. To hell with him.

It was just beginning to get light when we came to the creek, so we didn't have to argue about whether or not we were going to ride in the daylight. It was just a little stream, with the banks pretty well grown up in brush and salt cedars, and here and there a big green cottonwood. We rode along the bank for a while, looking for a place to stop. It looked like a good place for snakes, but not much of a spot for pitching camp. Finally we saw what we were looking for, a wide bend in the creek where the bank sloped down to the water, and the ground was brilliant green with new shoots of grass that was just beginning to come up. I didn't notice the horse until it was too late. It was a big black, with a white diamond in the middle of his forehead, grazing a big circle in the new green grass from the end of a picket rope. As we rounded the bend, the horse was the first thing we saw. But it didn't hold our attention long. The next thing we saw was the muzzle of a carbine.

I don't know how long I sat there looking at that gun before I realized that somebody had to be holding the thing. I don't suppose it was more than a small part of a second, but it seemed like a long time. By the time I was through looking at it, I knew everything about it.

It was a Ball magazine carbine, with the magazine under the barrel holding eight .50-caliber cartridges, loading from the rear. I had seen one or two of them before in cavalry officers' saddle boots. But guns like that didn't come easy, not even to cavalry officers. It was a beautiful piece of killing equipment. You could almost imagine that a man would be glad to get shot with a gun like that, if he cared anything for firearms. It had a tricky ramrod that pulled out the magazine spring to make loading fast and easy. Rim fire. It was a Yankee gun, but they hadn't brought it out in time to use it in the war, and I was glad of that. If they had, there would have been a lot more graves and a lot more boys sleeping under faded red flags with blue St. Andrew's crosses on them. I could almost tell, by looking at that carbine, what kind of man would be holding it.

The gun looked deadly, but quietly so. I figured the man would be the same. The gun didn't have an angry look or a belligerent look, but at the same time you knew it wouldn't stand for any foolishness. I wondered where the hell the owner had managed to get it, because I knew he wasn't a soldier, even before I looked at him.

And I was right. He was a long, hungry-looking man with faded gray eyes and a curious twist to his mouth that at first seemed like a smile, but after a second look you knew it wasn't. He had a face as long as a nightmare. His long, sharp nose drifted off to one side of his face, and there was a scar across the bridge, and a dent that you could lay the barrel of a .44 into. A week's growth of dirty gray beard didn't help his appearance any.

For clothes, he wore a hickory shirt with two buttons missing, a dirty bandanna around his scrawny neck, and a pair of serge pants slick from saddle wear. His hat had been black once, a long time ago, but it wasn't much of any color now.

I knew, before looking, that he would be wearing two side guns. I was right again. Two Colt .44's, the regular "Army" percussion model, but they had been altered to use metallic cartridges and looked like different guns. The ramrods and lever were gone, and new blued ejectors were molded to the sides of the barrels, and the new cylinders had loading gates. They were clean and cold and deadly-looking, and the gunsmith who had done the altering had been a man who loved his work.

I saw all this while maybe a tick of a second went by, while Red was rearing up just a little because of the jerk I had given on the reins. And by the time Red's forefeet hit the ground again I had the feeling that the stranger and I were old friends — or rather, old acquaintances, because he didn't look like the kind of man who would have many friends. I didn't know what Ray Novak was thinking, but I noticed that he didn't do anything foolish, like going for his own .44 or trying to ride the man down. There was something about the stranger that told you instinctively that a trick like that would only get you a sudden burial.

It crossed my mind quickly that maybe the stranger was a bounty hunter. The Yankees had plenty of such men working for them, free-lance killers who hunted fugitives from carpetbag law at so much a head. But I discarded that thought before it had time to form. This man wasn't working for the carpetbag law, or any other kind of law, for that matter. I don't know how I was so sure of that. He just wasn't the type.

"Ain't it kind of early in the morning," the man said softly, "to be taking a ride?"

"Or late at night," I said.

The stranger's mouth twitched slightly in

what was almost a nervous tic, and he made an almost silent grunting sound that came all the way up from his belly. It was like no sound I had ever heard before, but I was to find out later that it was laughter — or the closest thing to laughter that he ever came to. He hadn't asked us to raise our hands or drop our guns, so I figured that he didn't have anything against us in particular, except for the fact that we were strangers riding at an unusual hour.

I said, "We figured to make camp here on the bend, but I guess we can move on to another spot. . . ."

He made a negligent little motion with his shoulders. He had sized us up quickly as men not too friendly with the law. Why else would we be riding by night and sleeping by day? But he studied us for a while longer with that gray gaze of his. He regarded Red appreciatively, and the grub sack thoughtfully. I think it was the grub sack that made up his mind.

"I don't mind a bit of company . . . once in a while."

That, I knew, was all the invitation we were going to get. He lowered his carbine, holding it in the crook of his arm, and I started to swing down from the saddle.

Then Ray Novak spoke for the first time.

"We'll just move on," he said. "I reckon there are other places."

Ray hadn't taken to the stranger. Disapproval was stamped all over his face as he sat slouched in his saddle, his forehead screwed up in thought. Ray Novak had lived on law for so long that he recognized and hated outlaws instinctively. He was a special breed of man. Breeding, and blood lines, and training made his hackles rise at the sight of an outlaw, just as naturally as a long-eared Kentucky hound gets his back up at the sight of a badger. The fact that he was now an outlaw himself had nothing to do with it. He was still the son of Martin Novak.

I could see Ray thumbing back in his memory, going through all the dodgers on outlaws that had come through his pa's office, trying to place the stranger. He hadn't placed him yet. But sooner or later that plodding mind of his would come across the right dodger, and the right photograph or drawing, and the stranger would be pegged.

In the meantime, I didn't give a damn. I'd rather bed down with an outlaw than pull a stretch on the work gang. Anyway, I was tired of riding, and I was tired of Ray Novak. I dropped down from the saddle.

"If you want to ride on," I said, "you can ride. I'm stopping."

He didn't like that much. But he thought it over for a minute and didn't argue. Maybe he wanted to study the stranger some more. Or maybe he figured that all this was his fault in the first place and that made him bound to stay with me. I didn't know or care.

The stranger watched us carelessly as we unsaddled our horses and staked them around the bend near his big black. When we came back, he had a small fire going down near the water. He worked easily, almost lazily, selecting just the right kind of dry twigs. It was an expert fire, big enough to cook on, but practically no smoke came from it. He looked up and smiled that half-smile of his as I got the skillet out of the blanket roll and brought it and a bacon slab down to the fire. We were all friends, it seemed. But I noticed that he never let himself be maneuvered into a position that would show his back.

Before long, the sharp air of early morning was heavy with the rich smell of frying bacon. We propped the skillet over the fire on two rocks and once in a while I would turn the meaty slabs with a pocketknife. There is nothing like the smell of bacon in the early morning, but I was the only one that seemed to be interested. The stranger, I knew, was half starved, but he regarded the food only passively, hunkering down on his heels, with his back against the solid trunk of a cottonwood. Ray Novak hadn't said anything since we had unsaddled the horses, but I could see that he was still poking at the back of his mind, trying to get the man placed. I think the stranger saw it too. But he didn't seem to care.

We ate the bacon with Ma's cornbread, spearing the dripping slices with our pocket-knives, chewing and swallowing without a word. The stranger helped himself only after Ray and I had what we wanted. After we had finished, I went down to the creek and rinsed the skillet and filled it with fresh water. When I got back, the two of them were still sitting there on the ground, without saying a thing, staring thoughtfully at each other.

We boiled coffee in the skillet and I found two tin cups that Ma had packed in the blanket roll. I poured for Ray and myself, and still not a sound from anybody. I began to wonder what Ray Novak would do after he finally dug the stranger out of his memory. The stranger must have been wondering the same thing. And I had a crazy kind of feeling that the stranger was feeling sorry for Ray.

The coffee was black and strong and coated with a thin film of bacon grease. Like the bacon, the stranger had his coffee after Ray and I had finished. The silence was beginning to work on me. It magnified faraway sounds and brought my nerves out on top of my skin and rubbed them raw.

At last the stranger got slowly to his feet. "I'm much obliged for the grub," he said. "I guess I'll stretch out for a while. It's been a long night."

I said, "Sure." Ray Novak said nothing. The stranger walked up the slope a way, still not showing us his back, and stretched out under a rattling big cottonwood where his saddle was. He seemed to go to sleep, but there was no way of being sure about that. He pulled his hat partly over his face and lay down with his head on his saddle, but I had an uneasy feeling that he was just waiting.

I rinsed out the skillet and cups and put them back in the blanket roll. Ray had moved over to another cottonwood, still studying the stranger. Without looking at me, he said, "You'd better get some sleep, Tall."

"How about you?"

"I can stay awake for a while. I've got a feeling that one of us had better keep his eyes open."

The way he said it made me burn. It was in that off-hand sort of way — the way you'd tell a kid to go on to bed, you had important things to do. Maybe he thought my eighteen years made me a kid. Maybe, I thought, Ray Novak could go to hell.

But I didn't try to make anything of it. Beginning tonight, I didn't intend to ride with him any more. I spread my saddle blanket and sat leaning back against my saddle. I wasn't particularly sleepy, and, anyway, I wanted to see what Ray would do when he finally figured out who the stranger was.

Maybe fifteen minutes went by without either of us making a sound. Then, suddenly, Ray Novak made a little grunting noise and started to shove himself away from the cottonwood.

"All right," I said.

"All right what?"

"Who is our gun-loving friend? You've been working on it ever since he first stuck that carbine in our faces."

That took the wind out of him. "How did you know that?"

I shrugged. What difference did it make?

61

"Well, you were right," Ray said softly. "I should have figured it out a long time ago, but the beard and broken nose were things the government dodger on him didn't show. But I pegged him finally. He's Garret. Pappy Garret."

I didn't believe it at first. Pappy Garret was one of those men that you hear about all your life, but never see. The stories they told about him were almost as wild as the ones about Pecos Bill, or if you live in the north country, Paul Bunyan. He was wanted by both North and South during the war for leading plundering guerilla bands into the Kansas Free State. There wasn't a state in the Southwest that hadn't put a price on his head. Pappy Garret had the distinction of being probably the only thing in the world that the North and South saw alike on. They were out to get him.

Twenty notches was Pappy's record, as well as records of men like that could be kept. Some put the number of men who had gone down under Pappy's guns as high as thirty. But most claimed it was twenty, more or less, with some few claiming that he was overrated as a bad man and had never killed more than fifteen men in his life. No one, but Pappy Garret, would know for sure about that. And maybe Pappy didn't even know. The story was that he had a hideout up in the Indian Territory where he lived like a king by robbing the westbound wagon trains. Some people said that he lived with an Indian princess, the youngest daughter of the head chief of the Cheyennes. Others had it that he had been killed during the war fighting for the Confederacy — or the Union, depending on who was telling the story — and the real killer was Pappy Garret's son, a child of his by the Indian princess.

But most people didn't put much stock in that story. They figured that such a child couldn't be more than five or six years old, and a boy that age wasn't apt to be doing much killing. Not even a son of Pappy Garret's.

Still others had it that Pappy had gone to South America shortly after the war and was settled down there on a big plantation as respectable as you please, and all the killings that were laid to him were done by men who just happened to look a little like Pappy. Many such stories sprang up from time to time. Nobody really believed them, but it gave them something to talk about. The peace officers probably had the best idea of what Pappy was really like. He had killed two marshals on the Mexican border, and one up in the Panhandle country not long before, when they tried to arrest him. They saw Pappy Garret as a killer, without any fancy trimmings.

It was hard to believe that the lank, hungry-looking man not twenty yards away could be Pappy Garret, but Ray Novak didn't make mistakes about things like that. I knew one thing, however: Pappy hadn't been living like a king up in the Indian Territory, or anywhere else. He looked like he hadn't had a full belly since he was a child. Lying there with his eyes closed, with his head on the saddle, he looked more like a tired old man than a killer.

And maybe that was the reason I wasn't afraid of him. If I felt anything at all for Pappy Garret, it was sympathy. I'd had one night of running from the law, and that was plenty for me. I wondered how Pappy must feel after running for four or five years.

In the back of my mind, I realized that ten thousand dollars in bounty money was mine if I wanted it. All I had to do was dry my gun and empty it into Pappy Garret's skinny body and it was mine. There wouldn't even be any trouble when I rode back to John's City. The carpetbag law would be so glad to see Pappy's lifeless body dangling across that big black horse of his that they would forget the grudge they had against me. I'd be a hero, and a rich one at that. With ten thousand dollars, I could buy a piece of free range and have the beginnings of a ranch of my own. I could even marry Laurin Bannerman, which was what I wanted more than anything else.

But I didn't think I would be able to sleep at night without seeing that ugly, tired face of Pappy's; so the thought of killing him never really got to be an idea.

Ray Novak had ideas of his own. He stood up quietly, his hand unconsciously going down to his hip and feeling of the butt of his gun. I said, "Just what do you aim to do?"

There had never been a doubt in Ray's mind about what to do, after he had figured out who Pappy was. I don't think it was the bounty that set his mind for him. He probably never even thought of that. He just had too much law in him to let a killer like Pappy Garret lie there and do nothing about it. He glanced at me briefly, without saying anything. I guess he figured that my question wasn't worth answering.

I said, "Let him alone. He hasn't done anything to us."

Ray had his gun out now. He glanced at me curiously, and there were two small clicks as he pulled the hammer back. "Are you crazy?"

"We can saddle up and go our own way," I said. "Let the law catch him if they want him. What has the law ever done for us?"

"You *must* be crazy," Ray Novak said softly, not bothering to keep the scorn out of his voice. "Didn't you hear me? That man's Pappy Garret. He's killed twenty men. He'll kill that many more if somebody doesn't stop him. Stopping a man like that isn't just a job for the law. It's a job for every man who wants to live in peace, for every man who wants to see law and order come back to Texas."

I don't think I would have done anything if he hadn't made that speech, but when he got to talking about the right of law, and the wrong of outlaws, he got a holier-than-thou glint in his eyes like a camp-meeting preacher. Anyway, I was tired of Ray Novak. I was tired of his reverential respect for a tin sheriff's badge. I said, "Oh, hell, stop being so goddamn self-righteous!"

He looked as if I had kicked him in the gut while he wasn't expecting it. Over beneath the cottonwood, Pappy Garret stirred uneasily, and it occurred to me to wonder why a man like that would go to sleep in the company of two strangers.

66

Because he was asleep. There was no mistake about it now. Ray threw one quick angry glance in my direction — a glance that said that he was through with me, that from now on we could ride our separate ways.

"Very well, Tall," he said tightly. "I'll take care of it myself. You don't have anything to do with it."

"You're going to shoot him while he's asleep?"

"I'll take him any way I can. You don't give a mad dog a chance to protect itself, do you?"

All the talk had been in low whispers, but it was over now. Ray stepped out quietly, his gun at the ready. I could see what was going to happen. Ray would say something to wake Pappy — I knew he didn't have it in him to shoot a sleeping man. He would wake Pappy and Pappy would see how it was and try to get his guns. That would be the last move he would ever make. I had seen Ray handle guns and I knew Pappy Garret didn't have a chance.

I watched the sleeping gunman as those thoughts went through my mind. Pappy's face was relaxed now and I could see the deep lines of incredible weariness around his eyes and mouth. He looked as if he hadn't slept for days. I knew that he hadn't slept for years. Not real sleep. But now he lay like a log, numbed with weariness and comforted with hot food in his belly. He didn't look like a killer to me. He looked like an old man — very old and very tired — who couldn't hold his eyes open any longer.

Ray was coming up on Pappy's left, moving silently. In just a minute it would be over, if Pappy made a move for his guns. He would be able to sleep then — the long sleep that lasted forever.

The shout, when it came, startled me as much as anybody. It came high-pitched and loud and I hardly recognized it as my own.

"Pappy, look out!"

I lurched up to my feet. I don't know what I thought I was going to do then. It was too late to do anything but to stand there, half-crouched, and watch.

If I hadn't seen it I wouldn't have believed it. I never could entirely believe it when I watched Pappy handle guns. And you wouldn't believe that a man like Pappy could come awake as quick as he did, or that a man could move as fast. It all happened so fast that you couldn't be sure where the movement started and where it ended. He flipped over on his stomach and

68

rolled on his right side, and his right hand started plunging down to his holster before my first word was out. Ray was almost on top of him. His .44 was already out and cocked, and Ray was the man who could put two holes in a tossed-up can before it hit the ground. But by the time he got his second shot off this time, it was too late.

Ray Novak's first bullet slammed into Pappy's saddle, where his head had been only an instant before. Before he could thumb the hammer and press the trigger again, Pappy's own deadly .44 had bellowed. Pappy lay on his side, firing across his body. He must have drawn the gun and cocked it while he was flopping over, but it looked as if it had been in his hand all the time. One bullet was all he used.

I still hadn't moved. I stood there in that frozen half-crouch waiting for Ray Novak to go down. When Pappy fired only once, I knew it was over. He got to his knees and slowly lifted himself to his feet, darting a glance in my direction.

He said mildly, "Just unbuckle your pistol, son, and kick it over here."

I slipped the buckle on my cartridge belt and dropped it. Then I kicked it toward Pappy. But the thing that held me fascinated was Ray Novak. He was still standing. He wasn't even swaying. Then I saw that his gun hand was empty and I began to understand what had happened.

It hadn't been anything as fancy as shooting a man's gun out of his hand. Not even Pappy Garret could have done that, shooting as fast as he had, from the position he had been in. He had shot to kill, but the bullet had nicked Ray's forearm, making him drop the gun.

I lost any suspicion I had about Ray Novak's guts. He had plenty. There was nothing he could do now but stand there and wait for Pappy to finish him off. But he didn't flinch, or beg, or anything else. He just stood there, staring into those pale gray eyes of Pappy Garret's, while bright red blood dripped from his fingers and splashed in a little pool at his feet.

"What are you waiting on, Garret?" he said. "Why don't you go ahead and finish it?"

Pappy smiled that tired half-smile of his. He said softly, "I wouldn't waste another bullet on you. If I decide to kill you, I'll beat your brains out with a pistol butt. Now get the hell out of here before I do it."

Ray Novak's face burned a bright red. For a moment he didn't move. Then Pappy started toward him, slowly, holding his .44

70

like a club.

Ray said, "I'll get you, Garret. There won't always be carpetbag law in this country. And then I'll get you, if it's the last thing I do."

Pappy kept coming, half-smiling, with his pistol raised.

Ray turned then, and walked off, leaving a little trail of crimson in the tender green shoots of young grass. He didn't look at me. He walked on by. Around the bend he got his horse saddled, and pretty soon we heard him ride away.

I started to go myself. There was no explaining the reason I had yelled the way I had. Probably it had been because of a lot of things. Ray Novak and his everlasting talk of law. Ray Novak being able to put two bullets in a tin can. Even those rides of his over to Laurin's might have had something to do with it. All that, and Pappy lying there under the cottonwood, looking like a tired, helpless old man.

Anyway, I had done it. Ray Novak and I were through for good now, but I didn't give a damn about that. I turned and started up toward the bend in the creek to get Red saddled up.

But Pappy said, "Just a minute, son. I'd like to talk to you."

CHAPTER 3

I turned around. Pappy looked at me as he punched the empty cartridge out of his pistol and replaced it with a live round. After a moment he said:

"Thanks."

"Forget it. I wasn't trying to buy anything."

"You called me Pappy," he said. "How did you know who I was?"

"The other fellow figured it out. His old man used to be a town marshal and he saw your picture on one of the dodgers that came through the office."

Pappy shook his head, puzzled. "I know a man on the run when I see one. And he was on the run, the same as you. He didn't look like a marshal's son to me."

"His pa was marshal before the carpetbaggers took over."

Pappy began to understand. He rubbed a hand thoughtfully over his bushy chin. He moved back up the slope a few steps and sat down, leaning back with his elbows on his saddle. After a moment he untied the dirty bandanna and mopped his face and the back of his neck.

There was something about him that fascinated me. Only a minute ago he had come within a hair's breadth of getting a bullet in his brain, and all the emotion he showed was to wipe his face with a dirty handkerchief.

"Well," he asked, "what are you staring at?"

"You," I said. "I was just wondering how you came to go to sleep at a time like that."

He thought about that for a moment, and at last he sighed. "I was tired," he said simply. "I haven't slept for more than two days."

I should have saddled Red right then and rode away from there. There was trouble in the air. You could feel it all around, and you got the idea that trouble flocked to Pappy like iron filings to a lodestone. But I didn't move.

I said, "Ray Novak will be on your trail again. Sooner or later he'll be riding behind a marshal's badge, and when that happens he'll hunt you down. You should have killed him while you had the chance."

I half expected Pappy to laugh. The idea of Pappy having anything to fear from a youngster like Ray Novak would have been funny to most people. But Pappy didn't laugh. He studied me carefully with those pale gray eyes.

"A man does his own killing, son, and that's enough," he said. "I reckon if you want this Novak fellow dead, you'll have to see to it yourself."

I flared up at that.

"I don't care if he's dead or alive. Ray Novak doesn't mean anything to me."

Something changed in Pappy's eyes. I had an idea that way down deep he was smiling, but it didn't show on that ugly face.

"Maybe I spoke out of turn," he said finally. "I guess you're right. I should have killed him . . . while I had the chance."

There didn't seem to be any more to say. I turned and headed around the bend to where Red was picketed, and Pappy didn't make any move to stop me. But I could almost feel those eyes on me as I threw the double-rigged saddle up on Red's broad neck and began to tighten the cinches. I got my blanket roll and tied it on behind and I was ready to go. I was ready to leave this creek and Pappy Garret behind. I had enough trouble as it was, and if I got caught,

I didn't want it to be with a man like Pappy. I swung up to the saddle and pulled Red around to where the outlaw was still standing.

"I guess this is where I cut out," I said. "So long, Pappy."

"So long, son."

He looked a hundred years old right then. His heavy-lidded, red-rimmed eyes were watery with fatigue, and once in a while little nervous tics of sheer weariness would jerk at the corner of his mouth.

"Well," I said, "take care of yourself."

"The same to you, son," Pappy said. I started to pull Red around again and head downstream, when Pappy added, "Just a minute before you go."

He moved over a couple of steps to where his saddlebags were. He opened one of them and took out a pair of pistols, almost exactly like the ones he was wearing. Gleaming, deadly weapons, with rubbed walnut butts. He came over and handed them up to me.

"Bad pistols are like bad friends," he said. "They let you down when you need them most. You'd better take these."

I didn't know what to say. I looked at Pappy and then at the guns.

"Go on, take them," he said. "A fellow down on the border let me have them." And

75

he smiled that sad half-smile of his. "He wasn't in any condition to object."

I took the guns dumbly, feeling their deadly weight as I balanced them in my hands. I had never held weapons like them before. They had almost perfect balance. I flipped them over with my fingers in the trigger guards, and the butts smacked solidly in my palms, as if they had been carved by an artist specially to fit my hands.

I took a deep breath and let it out slowly. "All right, Pappy," I said finally. "You win."

He looked surprised. "I win what?"

"I'll keep watch while you catch some sleep. That's what you wanted, wasn't it?"

Then I saw something that few people ever saw. Pappy Garret smiled. Not that sad half-smile of his, but a real honest-to-God, face-splitting smile that reached all the way to his gray eyes.

"I think we'll get along, son," he said.

So that's the way it was. I unsaddled Red again and staked him out, then I took my position up on the creek bank while Pappy stretched out again with his head on the saddle. He raised up once to look at me, still slightly amused.

"My hide is worth ten thousand dollars at the nearest marshal's office," he said. "How do I know you won't try to shoot me while I'm asleep?"

"If I'd wanted ten thousand dollars that bad," I said, "I'd have killed you the first time you went to sleep. And I wouldn't have been polite enough to wake you up first. I don't let my conscience bother me, the way Novak does."

Pappy's mouth twitched, and there was that almost silent grunting sound, and I knew that he was laughing. He was dead asleep before his head hit the saddle again.

I had time to do some thinking while Pappy slept. I decided that maybe it wouldn't be a bad idea, after all, to stick with Pappy until we reached the Brazos. If anybody would know all the outtrails to miss the cavalry and police, Pappy Garret was the man. And avoiding cavalry and police was about the most important thing I could think of right now.

I didn't think much about Ray Novak. We had never been anything in particular to each other, and now that we were separated for good, I was satisfied. I didn't give a damn where he went or what he did.

But I thought of Laurin Bannerman. Laurin, with eyes a little too large for her small face, and her small mouth that always looked slightly berry-stained, and her laugh

77

that was as fresh as spring rain. I thought about her plenty now that I had time on my hands and there was nothing else to do. It was a funny thing, but I had never paid any attention to her until a couple of years ago. I guess that's the way boys are around that age. One minute girls mean nothing, and the next minute they're everything.

That was Laurin for me. Just about everything.

It was late in the afternoon when Pappy woke up. I was sitting under a cottonwood up on the creek bank, flipping my new pistols over and over to get the feel of them. Pappy sat up lazily, stretching, yawning, and scratching the mangy patches of beard on his face.

"That's better," he said. "Much better." He got up on his feet and hobbled around experimentally. "You handle those guns pretty good, son," he said. "Do you think you can shoot them as well?"

"Well enough, I guess."

Pappy shook his head soberly and beat some of the dust from his battered hat. "That's one thing no man ever does — shoot well enough. Sooner or later, if you keep looking, you'll find some bird that can slap leather faster."

"How about you?" I asked.

Pappy grinned slightly. "Maybe I haven't looked long enough," he said. "But I don't expect to live forever."

He began getting his stuff together, a ragged gray blanket that still had C.S.A. stenciled on it in faded black letters, a change of clothing, and that was about all. He did have some tobacco, though. He took the sack out of his shirt pocket and poured some of the powdery stuff into a little square of corn shuck, Mexican style, and tossed the makings up to me.

"You figure to ride east tonight?" he asked casually.

"That's what I had in mind."

"Alone?"

He was holding a match up to his cigarette and I couldn't see his face. "I guess that's up to you," I said.

He got that surprised look again. "How do you mean, son?"

He came up the slope and held a match while I got my cigarette to going. "Isn't that what you had in mind all along?" I said. "You look like a man that's just about played out. I don't know what you're running from, or how long you've been at it, but I know a man can't stay on the alert twenty-four hours a day, the way you must have been doing. I'm on my way to the

79

Brazos country. If you want to ride along and keep clear of the bluebellies, that's all right with me. We'll take turns sleeping and watching, and split up when we get to the river."

He tried to look all innocence, but he didn't have the face for it. "Do you think I'd let a mere boy tie up with a wanted man like me?"

"I think that's what you've been figuring on all along," I said.

I thought for a minute that he was going to break down and have a real laugh. But he didn't. He only said, "I guess we'd better get ready to ride. The sun will be down before long."

We made about twenty-five miles that night, and I knew before we had covered a hundred yards that I had picked the right man to get me through hostile country. Pappy knew every trick there was to learn about covering a trail. When a hard shale outcropping appeared, we followed it. When we crossed a stream we never came out near the place we went in. We even picked up the tracks of some wild cattle and followed them for two or three miles, mingling our own horses' hoofmarks with the dozens of others.

Pappy didn't ask me, but I told him about

myself as we rode. I even told him about Laurin, and Ray Novak, and how we came to be on the run, but there was no way of knowing what he thought about it. He would grunt once in a while, and that was all.

The next day, when we started to ride again, Pappy found a holster for me in one of those saddlebags of his. "Some people will tell you that a good shot doesn't need but one gun," he said, "but that's a lot of foolishness. Two of anything is better than one."

I felt foolish at first. It seemed like a lot of hardware — a lot more than an ordinary man needed to pack. But then, Pappy Garret wasn't an ordinary man, and when you were with Pappy you did as he did.

The day after that he said we didn't have to ride at night any more. He knew the country and there was nothing to worry about between us and the Brazos. Pappy, I gathered, was figuring on tying up with a trail herd headed for Kansas, but he never said so. He never said anything much after we got to riding, except for things like: "Loosen your cartridge belt, son. Let your pistols hang where your palms can brush the butts. Boothills are full of men that had to reach that extra inch to get their guns."

Or, at the end of a day maybe, when we were sitting around doing nothing: "Clean your pistols, son. Guns are like women; if you don't treat them right, and they turn against you, you've got nobody to blame but yourself."

It was almost sundown of the fourth day when we raised the wooded high ground with a sagging little log shack partly dug into the side of a hill. A thin little whisper of smoke was curling up from a rock chimney.

"It looks like they're expecting us," Pappy said, squinting across the distance.

I looked at him, and he saw the question before I could ask it. *"They"* he said "could be almost anybody. Anybody but the law, that is. The shack was built a long time ago by a sheepherder, but the cattlemen chased him out of Texas before he had time to get settled good. Some of the boys I know use it once in a while. I use it myself when I'm in this part of the country."

Well, I figured Pappy ought to know. We rode up toward the shack, and before long a man came out of it and stood there by the front door — the only door the cabin had — nursing what looked like a short-barreled buffalo gun. A Sharps maybe, about a .50 caliber, I guessed, when we got closer.

The man himself wasn't much to look at. About twenty-three or so, with a blunted, bulldog face, and long hair that hung down almost to his shoulders. His clothes were in about the same shape as Pappy's, and that wasn't saying much.

Pappy grunted as we pulled up near the crest of the hill. "It looks like one of the Creyton boys," he said.

I had a closer look at the man. The Creyton boys had hard names in Texas. They were supposed to have been in on a bank robbery or two down on the border. There were three of them: Buck, and Ralph, and a younger one called Paul. I figured the one at the shack was Paul Creyton, because he looked too young to have done the things that Buck and Ralph had to their credit.

The man recognized Pappy as we drew up into the thicket that passed for a front yard. I saw there was a lean-to shed on the side of the shack — a place for keeping horses, I supposed — but there was no horse stable there. The man lowered his gun and came forward.

"Pappy Garret," he said flatly, "I had an idea you was up in Kansas."

Pappy grinned slightly and leaned across his big black's neck to shake hands. "A Texan likes to see the old home place once in a while. How are you, Paul?"

The man glanced sideways at me, and Pappy said quickly, "This is Tall Cameron, a friend of mine. He's riding as far as the Brazos with me."

We nodded at each other. Paul Creyton said, "You haven't seen Buck, have you?"

"Not for about two years," Pappy said.

"We split up down on the Black River," Creyton went on flatly, as if he had gone over the story a hundred times in his mind. "A Morgan County sheriff's posse jumped us just south of the river. Ralph's dead. A sonofabitch gave him a double load of buckshot. My horse played out about four miles off, down in the flats, and I had to leave him in a gully."

I watched Pappy stiffen, just a little, then relax. "That's too bad about Ralph," he said softly.

"A double load of buckshot the sonofabitch gave him," Paul Creyton said again. "Right in the face. I wouldn't of known him, my own brother, if I hadn't been standing right next to him and seen him get it." His little eyes were dark with anger, but I couldn't see any particular grief on his face. He jerked his head toward the shack. "It ain't much, Pappy, but you and your friend are welcome to stay with me. I was just going out to see if I couldn't shoot myself some grub."

Pappy looked at me. We had been riding a long way and our horses needed a rest, but he was leaving the decision up to me.

"I've got some side bacon and corn meal," I said. "I guess that will see us through supper."

We cooked the bacon at a small rock fireplace in one corner of the shack, then we fried some hoecake bread in the grease, and finally made some coffee. Pappy and Paul Creyton talked a little, but not much. Somehow I gathered that Pappy wasn't such a great friend of the Creytons as I had thought at first.

After supper, it was almost dark, and the only light in the shack came from the little jumping flames in the fireplace. Talk finally slacked off to nothing, and Paul Creyton sat staring into the fire, anger written into every line of his face. Whatever his plans were, he wasn't letting us in on them. Whatever was in his mind, he was keeping it to himself.

Pappy got up silently and went outside to look at his horse. I followed him.

"What do you think about that posse?" I said. "Do you think they'll follow Creyton up to this place?"

Pappy shook his head, lifting his horse's

hoofs and inspecting them. "Not tonight. This place is hard to find if you don't know where to look, and Paul can cover a trail as well as the next one."

I rubbed Red down and gave him some water out of a rain barrel at the edge of the shack. His ribs were beginning to show through his glossy hide, and there were several briar scratches across his chest. But there wasn't anything wrong with him that a sack of oats or corn wouldn't fix.

I heard Pappy grunt, and I looked up. He had his horse's left forefoot between his knees, gouging around the shoe with a pocketknife.

"A stone bruise," he said. "He's been walking off center since noon, but I figured it was because he was tired." He got the rock that was caught under the rim of the shoe and flipped it out. "Well, there won't be any riding for a day or so, until that hoof is sound again."

"That means staying here tomorrow?"

"It means *me* staying here. You don't have to. Another day's ride will put you on the Brazos."

For a minute I didn't say anything. I hadn't figured that it would be any problem to pack up and leave Pappy any time I felt like it. But there was something about that ugly face that a man could get to like. He didn't have many friends. Maybe I was the closest thing to a friend that he had ever had. I made up my mind.

"I'll wait," I said. "We'll ride in together."

I imagined that I saw Pappy smile, but it was too dark now really to see his face. Then, without looking up, he said, "In that case, you'd better keep an eye on that red horse of yours."

"What is that supposed to mean?"

"If you were on foot," Pappy said, "and in no position to get yourself a horse, what would you do?"

"Like Paul Creyton."

"We'll say like Paul Creyton."

I began to get mad just thinking about it. "If he lays a hand on Red," I said, "I'll kill him."

Pappy turned, and stretched, and yawned, as if it were no concern of his. "Maybe I'm wrong," he said, "but I doubt it. He's got to have a horse, and that animal of yours is the closest one around."

He started back toward the shack, toward the doorway faintly jumping in orange firelight. "Just a minute," I said. "How are you so sure that he won't try to steal that black of yours?"

Pappy smiled. He was in the dark, but I

knew he was smiling.

"Paul Creyton knows better than to steal an animal of mine," he said.

When I got back to the shack I decided that Pappy had the whole thing figured wrong. Creyton had his blanket roll undone and was stretched out in front of the fireplace when I came in. He didn't look like a man ready to make a quick getaway on a stolen horse. Pappy was sitting on the other side of the room with his back to the wall, smoking one of his corn-shuck cigarettes.

"It seems like Paul just came from your part of the country," he said.

"John's City?"

Creyton sat up and worked with the makings of a cigarette. "That's the place," he said. "Me and Ralph and Buck came through there a few days back. About the day after you pulled out, according to what Pappy tells me."

I looked at Pappy, but his face told me nothing.

"Well, what about it?"

"Nothing about it," Creyton said bluntly. "We just came through it, that's all. The carpetbag law was raisin' hell. Stoppin' all travelers, police makin' raids on the local ranchers. All because some white punk took a swing at a cavalryman, they said."

I hadn't been ready for that. I had figured, like Ray Novak, that if the two of us got out of the country for a while it would all blow over. But here the police were raiding the ranches, because of us. Our own place, maybe. Or the Bannerman place, where Laurin was.

If one of the pigs so much as laid a hand on Laurin . . .

The thought of it made me weak and a little sick. I wheeled and started for the door.

"Where do you think you're going?" Pappy said.

"Back to John's City."

"Do you plan to go on foot? I don't care what you do with yourself, but I hate to see you kill a good horse out of damn foolishness. Wait till tomorrow. You'll make better time in the long run by giving your horse a rest."

Pappy was right. I knew that, but it wasn't easy staying here and wondering what might be happening to Laurin, or Ma and Pa, and doing nothing about it. Creyton got slowly to his feet, standing there in front of the fireplace, looking at me.

"You'd better listen to Pappy, kid," he said. "When you need a horse you need him bad. I ought to know."

I didn't want Creyton's advice. For all I knew, he just wanted me to stick around a while longer to give him a better chance to steal my horse. But I knew they were both right. Red had been pushed hard for the past few days, and if I tried to push him again tonight he might break down for good.

So I stayed. When the fire burned out, we made blanket pallets on the dirt floor, and before long Pappy's heavy breathing told me that he was asleep. He didn't snore. From time to time the rhythm of his breathing would break, he would rouse himself, look around, and then go back to sleep again. That was the way Pappy was. He never slept sound enough to snore. You had a feeling that he never let his mind be completely blanked out, that he always kept some little corner of it open. Being on the run had done that. He was afraid to allow himself the luxury of real sleep. A man like Pappy never knew when he would have to be wide awake and ready to shoot.

I lay awake for a long while, listening to a night wind moan and fling gravel and dust against the shack. Creyton seemed to be asleep. His breathing was regular, and once in a while he would snort a little and roll over on the hard ground. I lay there, with my eyes wide open, not taking any chances.

The night crawled by slowly. How many hours, I don't know. My eyes burned from keeping them open, and every so often I'd feel myself dropping off and I'd have to start thinking about something. I wanted a cigarette, but I didn't dare light one. I was asleep, as far as Paul Creyton was concerned, and I wanted to keep it that way in case he had ideas about that red horse of mine. I started thinking about Laurin.

I was dreaming of Laurin when something woke me. I didn't remember going to sleep, but I had. I sat up immediately, looking around the room, but it was too dark to see anything. I could hear Pappy's breathing. But not Paul Creyton's.

Sickness hit in my stomach, and then anger. Then, outside the shack, I heard Red whinny, and I knew that was the thing that had wakened me.

I went to the door, and in the pale moonlight I could see Paul Creyton throwing a saddle up on Red's back. So Pappy had been right all along. I found my cartridge belt on the floor, swung it around my middle and buckled it. Pappy didn't move. Didn't make a sound.

I didn't feel angry now, or in any particular hurry. I knew Creyton wasn't going to get away with stealing my horse, the same as that time, years ago, when I had known that Criss Bagley wouldn't hurt me with that club. I didn't know just how I would stop him; but I would stop him, and that was the important thing.

The night was quiet, and the sudden little scamper of Red's hoofs was the only thing to disturb it as I stepped out of the shack. Creyton had the horse all saddled and ready to ride by the time I got out to the shed. He was standing in the shadows, on the other side of Red, and I couldn't see him very well. But he could see me.

I never heard of a man talking his way out of horse stealing, and I guess Creyton never had either. Anyway, he didn't try it this time. He moved fast, jerking Red in front of him. Everything was so cut and dried that there wasn't any use thinking about it, even if there had been time. I dropped to my knees, with one of my new .44's in my hand. For just a moment I wondered how I was going to get Creyton without hitting Red. Then I made out the figure of Creyton kneeling under the horse's belly, and his gun blazed.

It all happened before Red could jump. I felt the .44 kick twice in my hand, the shots crowding right on top of Creyton's, and something told me there was no use wasting any more bullets. Red reared suddenly and, as he came crashing down with those ironshod hoofs, there was a soft, mushy sound, like dumping a big rock into a mud hole.

I thought for a minute that I was going to be sick. But that passed. I ran forward and caught hold of the reins and stroked the big horse's neck until he began to quiet down. There were nervous little ripples running up and down his legs and shoulders, but he got over his wild spell. I petted him some more, then led him away from the place and hitched him to a blackjack tree near the shack.

Paul Creyton was dead. I dragged him out into the moonlight and had a look at him. His face was a mess of meat and gristle and bone where Red's hoof had caught him, but that wasn't the thing that had done it. He had a bullet hole in the hollow of his throat, just below his Adam's apple, and another one about six inches up from his belt buckle. The one in the throat went all the way through, breaking his neck and leaving a hole about the size of a half dollar where the bullet came out. His head flopped around like something that didn't even belong to the rest of the body, when I tried to pick him up.

It had all happened too fast to make much of an impression on me at first. But now I was beginning to get it. I backed up and swallowed to keep my stomach out of my throat. I hadn't known that a man could die like that. Just a flick of the finger, enough to pull a trigger, and he's dead. As easy as that. The night was cool, almost cold, but I felt sweat on my face, and on the back of my neck. Sweat plastered my shirt to my back. I walked away from the place and headed back toward the shack.

It occurred to me to wonder what had happened to Pappy. He must have heard the shooting. The way he slept.

As I stepped through the doorway, a match flared and Pappy's face jumped out at me as he lit a cigarette. He put the match out and I couldn't see his face any more, just the glowing end of that corn-shuck tube, with little sparks falling every once in a while and dying before they hit the floor.

He said at last, "Creyton?"

"He's dead."

I could see the fire race almost halfway down the cigarette as he dragged deeply. I was still too numb to put things together. I only knew that Pappy had been awake at the time of the shooting and he had made no move to help me. He hadn't even bothered to come out and see if I was dead or not. He took one more drag on the cigarette and flipped it away.

"Well," he said, "it's just as well. Maybe I could have stopped it, but I doubt it. Sometimes it's best to let things run until they come out the way they're bound to in the end, anyway."

"Were you awake," I asked, "while he was trying to steal my horse?"

"I was awake."

"A hell of a friend you are! What was the idea of laying there and not even bothering to wake me up?"

"You woke up," Pappy said mildly. "Anyway, it wasn't any of my business. I did my part when I warned you about Paul Creyton. What if I had walked into the quarrel and shot Paul for you? What difference would it have made? He's dead anyway."

"But what if he had shot me?" I wanted to know.

I could almost see Pappy shrug. "That's the way it goes sometimes. By the way, you handle guns pretty well, at that. Paul Creyton wasn't the worst gunman in Texas, not by a long sight."

It took me a while to get it. But I had a good hold now. All the time I had been thinking that Pappy was my friend. He didn't even know what the word meant. Bite-dog-bite-bear, every man for himself, that was the way men like Pappy Garret lived. Unless, of course, some dumb kid came along who might be of some use to him for a few days. I'd played the fool all right, thinking that you could ever be friends with a man like that.

"Buck Creyton," I said. "You were afraid to take a hand with his kid brother because you knew you'd have Buck Creyton on your tail."

"I'll admit I gave Buck some thought in the matter," Pappy said.

I found that I still had the pistol in my hand. I flipped it over and shoved it in my holster. It's surprising how fast the shock of killing a man wears off. I wasn't thinking of Paul Creyton now. I was just thinking of how big a fool I had been, and getting madder all the time.

"This finishes us, Pappy. From now on you take your trail and I'll take mine. This is as far as we go together."

There was another flare of a match as Pappy lit a fresh cigarette. "Of course, son," he said easily. "Isn't that the way you wanted it all along?"

I left Pappy in the shack. I'd had enough of him. I went outside and gentled Red some more and wondered vaguely what to do with Paul Creyton. I didn't have any feeling for him one way or the other, but it didn't seem right just to leave him there.

What I finally did was to drag him down to the bottom of the slope and roll up boulders to build a tomb around him. That was the best I could do since I didn't have anything to dig a grave with. It was hard work and took a long time, but I stuck with it and did a good job. Anyway, it had a permanent look, and it would keep away the coyotes and buzzards.

When I finished, the sky in the east was beginning to pale, and it was about time to start riding back toward John's City. I stood there for a while, beside the tomb, half wishing I could work up some feeling for the dead man. A feeling of regret, or remorse, or something. But I didn't feel anything at all. I looked at the pile of rocks that I had rolled up, and it was hard to believe that a man was under them. A man I had killed.

When I started up toward the shack again, I saw that Pappy had come outside and had been watching the whole thing. There was a curious twist to his mouth, and a strange, faraway look in his eyes, as I walked past him. But he didn't speak, and neither did I.

I got Red saddled again, and, as I finished

tying on the blanket roll, Pappy came over.

"You probably don't want any advice," he said, "but I'm going to give you some anyway. Go on down to your uncle's place on the Brazos, like your old man wanted. You'll just get into trouble if you go back home and try bucking the police."

I swung up to the saddle without saying anything.

Pappy sighed. "Well . . . so long, son."

I had forgotten that I was still wearing the guns that he had given me, or I would have given them back to him. As it was, I just pulled Red around and rode west.

CHAPTER 4

Around the second day, on the trail back to John's City, I began to think straight again. I began to wonder if maybe Pappy hadn't been right again and I was acting like a damn fool by going back and asking for more trouble from the police. Maybe — but I had a feeling that wouldn't be wiped away by straight thinking. It was a feeling of something stretching and snapping my nerves like too-tight banjo strings. I couldn't place it then, but I found out later what the feeling was. It was fear.

Up until now it was just a word that people talked about sometimes. I always thought it was something a man felt when a gun was pointed at him and the hammer was falling forward, or when a condemned man stood on the gallows scaffold waiting for the trap to spring. But then I remembered that I hadn't felt it when Paul Creyton had taken a shot at me a few nights back. This was something new. And I couldn't explain it. When I felt it, I just pushed Red a little harder in the direction of John's City.

We made the return trip in three days, because I wasn't as careful as Pappy had been about covering my trail. We came onto the John's City range from the north, and I made for the Bannerman ranch first because it was closer than our own place, and I wanted to see if Laurin was all right. I remember riding across the flat in the brilliant afternoon, wondering what I would do if the cavalry or police happened to be waiting for me there at the Bannermans'. I had been around Ray Novak and his pa enough to be familiar with the law man's saying: "If you want to catch a fugitive, watch his woman."

But I didn't see anything. I raised the chimney of the Bannerman ranch house first, sticking clear-cut against the ice-blue sky. And pretty soon I could make out the whole house and the corrals and outbuildings, and that feeling in my stomach came back again and told me that something was wrong.

It was too quiet, for one thing. There are sounds peculiar to cattle outfits — the sound of blacksmith hammers, the rattle of wagons, or clop of horses — sounds you don't notice particularly until they are missing. There were none of those sounds as I rode into the ranch yard.

And there were other things. There were no horses in the holding corrals, and the barn doors flapped forlornly in the prairie wind, and the bunkhouse, where the ranch hands were supposed to be, was empty. The well-tended outfit I had seen a few days before looked like a ghost ranch now. And, somehow, I knew it all tied up with that feeling I had been carrying.

I rode Red right up to the back door and yelled in.

"Laurin! Joe! Is anybody home?"

It was like shouting into a well just to hear your voice go round and round the naked walls, knowing that nobody was going to answer.

"Laurin, are you in there?"

Joe, the old man, the ranch hands, they didn't mean a damn to me. But Laurin . . .

I didn't dare think any further than that. She was all right. She had gone away somewhere, visiting maybe. She *had* to be all right.

I dropped down from the saddle, took the back steps in one jump, and rattled the back door.

"Laurin!"

I hadn't expected anything to happen. It was just that I didn't know what else to do. I was about to turn away and ride as fast as I could to some place where somebody would tell me what was going on here. Something was crazy. Something was all wrong. I could sense it the way a horse senses that he's about to step on a snake, and I wanted to shy away, just the way a horse would do. I took the first step back from the door, when I heard something inside the house.

It moved slowly, whatever it was. Not with stealth, not as if it was trying to creep up on something. More as if it was being dragged, or as if it was dragging itself. Whatever it was, it was coming into the kitchen, toward the back door where I still stood. Then I saw what it was.

"Joe," I heard myself saying, "my God, what happened to you?"

He was hardly recognizable as a man. His face had been beaten in, his eyes were purplish blue and swollen almost shut. His mouth was split open and dried blood clung to his chin. Blood was caked on his face and in his hair and smeared all over the front of his shirt.

"What are you doing here?" he asked

dully. I noticed then that his front teeth were missing. But I only noted it in passing. In the back of my mind. I could think of only one thing then — Laurin.

I jerked the screen door open and went inside. "Joe, where's Laurin? Is she all right?"

He looked at me stupidly and I grabbed the front of his shirt and shook him.

"Answer me, goddamn you! Where's Laurin?"

He shook his head dumbly and began to sag. I held him up and pulled a kitchen chair over with my foot and let him sit down.

"So help me God," I said, "if you don't tell me what happened to Laurin I'll finish what somebody else started."

He worked his mouth. I couldn't tell if he understood me or not. It took him a long time to get a sound out. He worked his mouth, rubbed his bloody face, licked his split lips.

Then, "Laurin . . ." he said finally. "She's . . . all right."

I realized that I had been holding my breath all the time it had taken him to get those words out. Now I let it out. It whistled between my teeth, and my heart began to beat and blood began to flow. Relief washed over me like cool water on a hot day.

"Where is she, Joe? Tell me that."

He started to get up, then sat down again. He made meaningless motions with his hands. Whoever had worked on him had done a hell of a good job. I wondered if maybe there wasn't a hole in the back of his head where all his brains had leaked out.

"Answer me, Joe! Where is she? Where is Laurin?"

"Your place," he managed at last. "Your place . . . with your ma."

I didn't stop to wonder what Laurin would be doing at our ranch. I was too relieved to wonder about anything then. Joe started to stand up again and I pushed him down.

"Stay where you are," I said. "I'll get you some water."

I found a bucket of water and a dipper and a crock bowl on the kitchen washstand. Then I got some dish towels out of the cupboard and brought the whole business over and put it on the kitchen table. I wet the towel and wiped some of the blood off his face. I squeezed some water over his head and cleaned a deep scalp wound behind his ear. That was about all I could do for him. He didn't look much better after I had finished, but he seemed to feel better.

I gave him a drink out of the dipper and said, "Can you talk now?"

He touched his mouth gently, then his eyes and nose. "Yes," he said. "I guess I can talk."

"What happened to you?" I asked. "What happened out there?" I motioned toward the empty corrals and barns and bunkhouse out in the ranch yard.

"The police," he said. "The goddamned state police. They came here yesterday morning wanting to know where you were. When we didn't tell them, they ran off all the livestock — that's where the hands are, looking for the cattle. They threatened to burn the place if we didn't tell them. They're mad. Crazy mad. That bluebelly that Ray gave the beating to was the governor's nephew, or cousin, or something, and all hell's broke loose in John's City. They're out to get every man that ever said a word against the carpetbag rule. They want you especially bad, I guess."

"Why do they want me so bad? Hell, I wasn't the one that hit the governor's kinfolks."

"Because you're the only one that got away from them," Joe Bannerman said. "Ray Novak came back and gave himself up. But they're not satisfied. They got to

105

thinking about that fight you had a while back. They won't be satisfied until they've got you on the work gang, right alongside of Ray Novak."

So Ray Novak had come back. Gave himself up to carpetbag law. It didn't surprise me the way it should have. Maybe I knew all along that sooner or later all of that law-and-order his old man had pounded into him would come to the top. Well, that was all right with me. He could put in his time on the work gang if he wanted to, but not me. Not while I had two guns to fight with.

Joe Bannerman was studying me quietly, through those purple slits of eyes. Something was going on in that mind of his, but I couldn't make it out at first. There was something about it that made me uneasy.

"The police," I said, "they came back today to have another go at finding out where I'd gone. Is that how you got that face?"

He nodded and looked away. It hit me then, and I knew what it was about his eyes that worried me. For some crazy reason, Joe Bannerman was feeling sorry for me. That wasn't like him. Refusing to give information to the bluebellies was different — any honest rancher would have done the same thing — but that look of sympathy — I hadn't been ready for that. Not from Joe Bannerman.

He said, "Tall, have you been home yet?"

"Not yet," I said. "I wanted to make sure that Laurin was all right."

He looked at his hands as if there was something very special about them. As if he had never seen another pair just like them before.

"I thought maybe you knew," he said. "I figured maybe that was the reason you came back."

I looked at him. "You thought I knew what?"

"About your pa."

"Goddammit, Joe, can't you come out and tell something straight, without breaking it into a hundred pieces? What about Pa?"

Then he lifted his head and he must have looked at me for a full minute before he finally answered.

"Tall, your pa's dead."

I don't know how long I stood there staring at him, wanting to curse him for a lousy liar, and all the time knowing that he was telling the truth. That was the answer to the feeling I'd had. It all made sense now. Pa, a part of me, had died.

Somehow I got out of the house. I remember Joe Bannerman saying, "Tall, be careful. There's cavalry and police everywhere."

I punished Red unmercifully going across the open range southeast toward our place. I rode like a crazy man. The sensible part of my brain told me that there was no use taking it out on Red. It wasn't his fault. If it was anybody's fault, it was my own. But the burning part of my brain wanted to hit back and hurt something, as Pa had been hurt, and Red was the only thing at hand.

But all the wildness went away the minute our ranch house came into sight, and there was nothing left but emptiness and ache. There were several buggies and hacks of one kind or another sitting in front of the house, and solemn, silent men stood around in little clusters near the front porch. I swung Red around to come in the back way, and the men didn't see me.

I didn't see any police. All the men were ranchers, friends of Pa's. The womenfolk, I knew, would be inside with Ma. As I pulled Red into the ranch yard, Bucky Stow, one of our hands, came out of the bunkhouse. When he saw who it was, he hurried toward me in that rolling, awkward gait that horsemen always have when they're on the ground.

"Tall, for Christ's sake," he said, "you

oughtn't to come here. The damn bluebellies are riled up enough as it is."

I dropped heavily from the saddle and put the reins in his hands. I noticed then that I had brought blood along Red's glossy ribs where I had raked him hard with my spur rowels, and for some crazy reason that made me almost as sick as finding out about Pa. Pa had loved that horse.

But I slapped him gently on the rump and he seemed to understand. I said, "Give him some grain, Bucky. All he wants."

"Tall, you're not going to stay here, are you?"

I left him standing there and headed toward the house. I went into the kitchen where two ranch wives were rattling pots and pans on the kitchen stove. They looked up startled, as I came in. I didn't notice who they were. I went straight on through the room and into the parlor where the others were.

The minute I stepped into the room everything got dead quiet. Ma was sitting dry-eyed in a rocker, staring at nothing in particular. Laurin was standing beside her with a coffee pot in one hand, holding it out from her as if she was about to pour, but there was no cup. She stared at me for a moment. Then, without a word, she began getting the other women out of the room.

In a minute the room was empty, except for just me and Ma. I don't believe it was until then that she realized that I was there. I walked over to her, not knowing what to do or say. When at last she looked up and saw me, I dropped down and put my head in her lap the way I used to do when I was a small boy. And I think I cried.

One of us must have said something after that, but I don't remember. After a while one of the ranch wives, well meaning, came in from the kitchen and said timidly:

"Tall, hadn't you better eat something?"

It was so typical of ranch wives. If there's nothing that can possibly be done, they want to feed you. Ma would have done the same thing if she had been in the woman's place.

I got to my feet and said, "Later, not now, thank you." The words sounded ridiculous, like somebody turning down a second piece of cake at a tea party. And out there somewhere Pa was dead.

The woman disappeared again, and I touched Ma's head, her thin, gray hair. "Ma . . ." But I didn't know how to go on. I wasn't any good at comforting people. And besides, she was still too numb with shock to understand anything I could say to her.

As I stood there looking at her, the ache and emptiness in my belly began to turn to quiet anger. Slowly, I began to put things together that I had been too numb to think about before. Instinctively, I knew that Pa hadn't died in any of the thousand and one ways a man could die around a ranch. He had been killed. I didn't know by whom, but I would find out. And when I did . . .

Ma must have sensed what I was thinking. She looked up at me with those wide, dry eyes of hers. She noticed the two .44's that I had buckled on, and I saw a sudden stark fear looking out at me.

"Tall . . . no! There's nothing you can do now. There's nothing you can do to bring him back."

But that anger that had started so quietly was now a hot, blazing thing. I heard myself saying:

"He won't get away with it, Ma. Whoever it was, I'll find him. Texas isn't big enough for him to hide where I can't find him. The world isn't that big. And when I do find him . . ."

That helplessness and terror in her eyes stopped me. She looked at me, and kept looking at me, as if she had never seen me before. I should have kept my thoughts to myself, but it was too late to change that now.

"Ma," I said, "don't worry about me."

But she didn't say anything. She just kept looking at me.

I went back to the kitchen and motioned to one of the ranch wives. "Would you mind looking after Ma for a while?" I asked. "I want to go outside for a minute, where the men are."

"Of course, Tall." She was a tremendous, big-bosomed woman, holding a steaming coffee pot in her hand. She had that same look of sympathy in her eyes that I had noticed with Joe Bannerman, and I hated it.

I went out the back way instead of the front, where I would have to pass through the parlor again and face that look of Ma's. Jed Horner was the first man I saw, a small rancher to the south, down below the arroyo. He and Cy Clanton were talking quietly near the end of the front porch. Neither of them seemed especially surprised to see me. They came forward solemnly to shake hands, something they never would have bothered about if Pa had been alive.

"We guessed that you'd be comin' back, Tall," Jed Horner said soberly, "as soon as you got the word."

"I guess you know all about it, don't you?" Cy Clanton asked.

"I don't know anything," I said, the words coming out tight. "But I'd like to know."

The two men nodded together, both of them glancing curiously at my two pistols. Then I noticed something strange for a gathering like this. All the men were armed, not only with the usual side guns, but some of them with shotguns and rifles.

"It was the police," Horner said. "Some damned white trash from down below Hooker's Bend somewhere. It seems like all the Davis police in Texas have congregated here at John's City. They claim they're goin' to teach us ranchers to be Christians if they have to kill half of us doin' it." Then he patted the old long-barreled Sharps that he held in the crook of his arm. "But we've got some idea about that ourselves."

"About Pa," I said. "I want to know how it happened."

"The police, like I said," Horner shrugged. "There must have been about a dozen of them, according to your ma. They started pushin' your pa around, tryin' to make him tell where you'd gone, and one of them hit him with the barrel of his pistol. That, I guess, was the way it happened."

"The funeral was yesterday," Cy Clanton

said. "We buried him in the family plot, in the churchyard at John's City. There wasn't a better man than your pa, Tall. If the police want a war, that's what they're goin' to get."

The anger was like a knife in my chest. The other men drifted over one and two at a time until I was completely surrounded now. Their eyes regarded me soberly.

I said, "Does anybody know the one that did it? The one that swung the pistol?"

Pat Roark, a thin, sharp-eyed man about my own age, said, "I heard it was the captain of the Hooker outfit. It seemed like he was a friend of that carpetbagger you gun-whipped a while back. Name of Thornton, I think."

I knew what to do then. I turned to Bucky Stow, who had sidled in with the group of men. "Bucky, cut out a fresh horse for me, will you? I guess I'll be riding into John's City."

There was a murmur among the men. A sound of uneasiness. "Don't get us wrong, Tall," Jed Horner said. "We're behind you in whatever you decide to do about this. Like I said, there wasn't a better man than your pa. But I think you ought to know it would be taking an awful chance riding right into town that way. Police are thick as lice on a dog's back."

I turned on him. "You don't have to go with me. It's my job and I can take care of it myself."

"Tall, you know we don't mean it that way. If that's what you want, why, I guess you can count on us to be with you."

The other men made sounds of agreement, but a bit reluctantly. Then a man I hadn't noticed before pushed his way to the front. He was a small man with a ridiculously large mustache, and dark, intelligent little eyes peering out from under bushy gray eyebrows. He was Martin Novak, Ray Novak's father.

"Don't you think you ought to think this over, Tall?" he asked quietly. "Is it going to settle anything if you and the other ranchers go riding into town, looking for a war?"

"I'm not asking anybody to go with me," I said.

He regarded my two pistols, and I wondered if Ray had told him about Pappy Garret. But those eyes of his didn't tell me a thing. Then he seemed to forget me and turned slowly in a small circle, looking at the other men.

"Why don't you break it up?" he asked quietly. "Go on home and give things a chance to straighten out by themselves. It'll just make things worse — somebody else will get killed — if you all go into town looking for trouble." Then he turned back to me. "Tall, you're wanted in these parts by the law. These other men will be breaking the law, too, if they tie up with you in this thing. Sooner or later there'll be real law in Texas. When that happens, this man Thornton will get what's coming to him. I'll give you my word on that."

He actually meant every word of what he was saying. He had lived law for so long that anything that walked behind a tin badge got to be a god to him.

"Do you expect me to do like your son?" I asked tightly. "Would you want me to give myself up to the bluebellies, after what they have just done here?"

He started to say something, and then changed his mind. He looked at me for a long moment, then, "I guess it wouldn't do any good to tell you what I think, Tall. You'd go on and do things your own way."

He turned and walked through the circle of ranchers. I heard Pat Roark saying, "Well, I'll be damned. I never figured the marshal would back down on his own people when it came to a fight with the bluebellies."

Then Bucky Stow came out of the barn leading a saddled bay over to where we were. Slowly, the circle begin to break up and the men went, one and two at a time, to get their horses.

I said, "Thanks, Bucky," as I took the bay's reins. "Take good care of Red. I'll want him when I get back."

Bucky shuffled uncomfortably. He was a quiet man who never said much, and I'd never known him to carry a gun, much less use one. He said, "Tall, I guess you know how I felt about your pa. I'd be glad to . . ."

"You stay here, Bucky. You look after the womenfolks."

His eyes looked relieved. I led the bay over toward the corral where the ranchers were getting their horses cinched up. I hadn't taken more than a dozen steps when Laurin came out on the front porch.

"Tall?"

I wasn't sure that I wanted to talk to Laurin now. There was only one thing in my mind — a man by the name of Thornton. But she called again, I paused, and then I went over to the end of the porch. Her eyes had that wide, frightened look that I had seen in Ma's eyes a few minutes before.

"Tall," she said tightly, "don't do it. They'll kill you in a minute if you go into town looking for trouble."

I tried to keep my voice even. "Nothing's going to happen to me. You just stay here

117

and take care of Ma. There's nothing to worry about."

She made a helpless little gesture with her hands. Even through all the bitterness that was in me, I thought how beautiful she was and how much I loved her.

"Tall, please, for my sake, for your mother's sake, don't do anything now."

"I have to do something," I said. "Don't you see that?"

"I just know that there's going to be more trouble, and more killing. It will be the start of a war if you go into town bent on revenge."

I tried to be patient, but there was something inside me that kept urging me to strike out and hurt. I said, "What do you want me to do, turn yellow like Ray Novak, and turn myself over to the bluebellies?"

"It wouldn't be turning yellow, Tall." Her voice was breathless, the words coming out fast, stumbling over each other in their haste. "Tall, can't you see what you'll be starting? If you can't think of yourself, think of others. Of me, and your mother."

The ranchers were waiting. They had their horses saddled, and the only thing holding them up was myself. I started backing away. "This is man's business," I said. "Women just don't understand things like this." Then

I added, "Don't worry. Everything's going to be all right." But the words sounded flat and stale in my own ears.

We rode away from the ranch house with me in the van, and Pat Roark riding beside me. There was about a dozen of us, and we rode silently, nobody saying a word. I concentrated on the thud of the bay's hoofs, and the little squirts of powdery red dust that rose up, and a lazily circling chicken hawk up above, cutting clean wide swaths against a glass sky. I didn't dare to think of Pa. There would be time enough for that.

We traveled south on the wagon road that we always used going to Garner's Store, across the arroyo and onto the flats. We reached Garner's Store, a squat boxlike affair made of cottonwood logs and 'dobe bricks, about an hour after leaving the ranch house. It set in the V of the road, where the wagon tracks leading from the Bannerman and the Novak ranches came together. As we sighted the store, we saw two Negro police leave in a cloud of dust, heading south toward John's City.

There was no use going after them. A dozen armed men couldn't very well ride into town and expect to surprise anybody. We pulled our horses up at the store and let them drink at the watering trough. After a while Old Man Garner came out looking vaguely worried.

I said, "Those were Davis police, weren't they, the ones that fogged out of your place a few minutes back?"

The old man nodded. "I guess they was kind of expectin' something out of your pa's friends, Tall. Anyway, they stayed here until they saw you comin', and then they lit out for town."

Pat Roark said, "Did they mention what outfit they was out of?"

The old man thought. "They mentioned Hooker's Bend. I reckon they come from around there."

Pat looked at me. "You ready to ride, Tall?"

"I'm ready."

CHAPTER 5

As we rode, Pat Roark seemed to be the only man in the whole group who was completely at ease. He rode slouched over to one side of his saddle, grinning slightly, as if he was looking forward to the excitement. He's just a kid, I thought. Nothing but a damned green kid who doesn't know what he's getting into. But then I realized that he was as old as I was. Maybe a few months older. I'd never thought of him before as being a kid.

"Cavalry," Pat Roark said, as if he had been giving it considerable thought. "They're the ones we've got to watch out for. The police don't amount to a damn."

"How much cavalry is there?" I asked.

He shrugged. "There's a detail up north somewhere, about a half a troop, I think. They come and go in John's City, but they've got too much territory to cover to stay there all the time."

"But the police will be there," I said.

He looked at me. "They'll be there. This Thornton I mentioned — Jake Thornton, I think his name is — probably we'll find him in the City Bar. It's the only place in town that caters friendly to carpetbaggers."

I kept my voice level. "Do you know this Thornton when you see him?"

"I know him. I'll point him out to you when the time comes. It'll be a pleasure."

I knew then that Pat Roark was the only one I could really depend on when things got down to shooting. The others, mostly, were just coming along because they didn't have the guts to stay back. They were all good men, and I didn't have anything against them, but this was my fight, not theirs, and they knew it better than anybody.

When we sighted the town, Pat took out his pistol to check the loading. I said, "Do you mind if I look at that?" He grinned and handed it over.

It wasn't much of a weapon — an old .36-caliber Cofer revolver. It was mounted on a brass frame and had a naked trigger without any guard. I recognized it as one of the guns that the Confederacy had bought from some outlaw arms dealers before the war, probably because the Yankees were afraid to shoot them and they were cheap. Across the top of the frame and barrel there was the mark: T. W. Cofer's Patent, Portsmouth, Va. I figured it was about an even bet that the cylinder would explode before you could get off the third shot.

I handed the pistol back to him. Then, on impulse, I drew one of those new deadly .44's that Pappy had given me and handed that over too.

"You'd better take this," I said, "in case you need a pistol."

He took it, admiring its velvety finish and fine balance. Then he grinned again and shoved it into his waistband. "Thanks, Tall. I guess with a pair of these between us, we haven't got anything to worry about."

In Pat Roark, I knew that I had one good man on my side. And one good man was all I needed.

We rode into Main Street in no particular formation, Pat and myself still in the van, and the others strung out in the rear. The town was ready for us. Everything that a bullet could hurt had been taken off the plank walk and dragged inside. The street was almost deserted, with only two or three horses standing at the block-long hitching rack. The last buckboard was just pulling out of the far end of the street as we came into town.

"We hit it right," Pat Roark said out of the side of his mouth. "The cavalry's not in town." He was moving his head slowly from side to side, not missing a thing. The thumb of his right hand, I noticed, was hooked in his cartridge belt, close to the butt of that new .44. When his head turned in my direction again he said, "You want to try the City Bar first?"

I nodded. The bar was a two-story frame building standing on the corner, at the end of the block. When we reached it, I motioned for Pat to pull in, and I waited for the others to come up.

"Look," I said, as they grouped up around me, "I know this is none of your fight. I'm not asking you to come in with me, but I'll appreciate it if you keep watch outside here and see that nobody has a chance to get me and Pat in the back."

The men looked as if they wanted to object and join in on the fight, but nobody did. Jed Horner was the only one to say anything.

"Tall, we don't want you to get the idea that we're not with you. It's just like I said . . ."

I left him talking and looped the bay's reins over the hitching rack. Pat was waiting for me on the plank walk, his back against

124

the building.

"I guess we might as well go in," I said.

"I guess so."

We kicked both batwings open at the same time and stepped inside. I was ready to draw from the first. I half expected a rifle, or maybe a shotgun, to be looking at us from over the bar. But there was nothing out of the way. Business was going on as usual. A couple of Davis policemen were having beer at the bar, a handful of turncoats and scalawags were in the back of the place where the gambling tables were. A roulette ball rattled like dry bones as the wheel spun, then the rattling stopped abruptly as the ball went into a slot. "Black, twenty-three," I heard somebody say.

"He isn't here," Pat said under his breath.

The bartender and two policemen were watching us carefully, but nobody made a move. There was something about the whole setup that I didn't like. I knew the bartender recognized me, and probably the two policemen as well. Then why didn't they do something? I was the one they wanted.

I went over every inch of the place with my eyes. There were nine men in the place, counting the bartender, a croupier, and a blackjack dealer. In the back of the place there were some stairs leading up to a small gallery jutting out over the gambling area, but there was nobody up there that I could see.

Without turning his head, Pat said, "You want to try the marshal's office?"

That would be the logical thing to do, but there was still something about this place that I didn't like. I walked over to the bar, and Pat stayed where he was, by the door. The roulette ball didn't rattle any more. The blackjack dealer paid off, raked his cards in, and waited. Everybody seemed to be waiting for something.

The bartender moved away from his two police customers and came down to the end of the bar where I was.

"What'll you have, Tall?" he asked easily. Maybe a little too easily.

"Information," I said. "I'm looking for a man. A man by the name of Thornton."

He thought it over carefully. "You ought to try the marshal's office," he said finally. "That's his headquarters, not here."

He started to reach under the bar for something. A bar rag maybe, or some fresh glasses. But it could have been a shotgun.

I said, "Just keep your hands where I can see them." The two policemen were watching us, but so far they hadn't made any move toward their guns. One was short and big around the belly and hips. The other was big all over, maybe six feet tall and weighing around two hundred pounds. I called down the bar.

"You down there, where's your captain?"

The big one set his glass down. He looked at the short, fat one, and they both grinned quietly, as if they were enjoying a secret little joke just between the two of them.

"Down at the marshal's office, I reckon," the big one said.

He was lying. I was sure of that without knowing how I was sure. I could have killed him right there, both of them, with no regrets, no feeling at all. It could just as easily have been one of them, I thought. I'd never be able to look at a policeman again without thinking that, without feeling that sick anger blaze up and burn again.

And the two of them stood there grinning. The bartender and the others didn't do anything.

I heard myself saying, "Do you know who I am?"

The big man shrugged. The short one had another go at his drink.

"The name is Cameron," I said. "Tall Cameron. I hear you Davis police are looking for me."

They didn't even blink. I was hoping that

they would make a move for their guns, but they didn't move at all.

The big man spoke mildly. "You must of heard wrong, kid. We don't want you."

"You're a goddamned liar," I said.

That jarred them for a minute. I watched the grins flicker and fade. They looked like they might go for their guns after all, and I was hoping they would. I was praying that they would give me an excuse to put a bullet . . . But that was as far as the thought went. Pat Roark stopped all thinking, all action that might have taken place, with:

"Tall, look out!"

I wheeled instinctively. I vaguely noticed that the bartender's hands had darted under the bar again and I caught the glint of a brutish sawed-off shotgun. And I was aware of the two police clawing for their own side guns — but all that was in the back of my mind. It was the gallery that held my attention.

The man up there had a rifle pointed at my chest. I didn't know how he got up there. Probably he had been up there all the time, waiting for me to turn my back. I knew, with the same instinct that told me the big policeman was lying, that the rifleman was Thornton. Before I had half whirled about I heard Pat Roark's .44 crash and saw the bartender sliding down behind the bar, the shotgun dropping from his limp fingers. Somehow my own gun was in my hand.

At a time like that you don't stop to think. Your mind seizes all the facts in a bunch and there is no time to separate them and decide where to act first. The two policemen were still clawing for their pistols, awkwardly. But the man on the gallery didn't have to draw. The rifle was ready, aimed, and I imagined that I could see the hammer falling. I forgot about the two policemen. The .44 bucked twice in my hand and the room jarred with the roaring. Two shots, I knew, would have to do it. I couldn't wait to see if the man would fall. The two policemen were awkward with pistols, but they weren't that awkward.

By the time I swung on them again, the big man's gun was just clearing his holster. I shot him in the belly and he slammed back against the bar, clawing at the neat black hole just above his belt buckle. The fat one didn't have a chance. He shouldn't have been allowed to carry a gun. He didn't know what to do with one. He was still fumbling with the hammer as my bullet buried itself in the flabby folds of fat under his chin. He reeled back and blood began to come out of his mouth.

It all happened in a second. Two seconds at the most. I stood there watching the fat man die. He sagged, clutching at the bar to hold himself up. But his fingers missed and he hit the floor with his back, kicked once or twice, and lay still.

Pat Roark shouted, "The door, Tall. I'll keep them covered while you back out."

But it wasn't over yet. Thornton, the man on the gallery, was still alive. He was on his knees clutching his middle, and bright red blood oozed between his fingers. I counted my shots in my mind. Two at Thornton, one at the big man, and one at the fat one. That was four. I had one bullet left. A six-shooter is actually a six-shooter only for fools and dime novels. There's always an empty chamber to rest the hammer on when the pistol is in the holster. I leveled the pistol at Thornton and fired my last bullet. I thought, This one's for you, Pa. It's too late to do you any good, but it's the only thing I know to do.

Thornton came crashing down from the gallery, falling across a poker table like a rag doll, then dumping into a shapeless heap on the floor.

I stood there breathing hard, the empty pistol still in my hand.

Pat said, "Tall, for God's sake, come on!"

But I waited a few more seconds, almost hoping that Thornton would move again so I could go over and beat the life out of him, the way he had done with Pa. But he didn't move. His eyes had that fixed glassy stare that always means the same thing. I had done all I could do.

The spectators — the carpetbaggers, and white trash, and scalawags — still hadn't moved. Their faces were pale with shock as they stared at the lifeless figures on the floor. That wasn't the way they had expected it to work out. They had been confident that their man could kill me easily from his place on the gallery, but now that it hadn't worked out that way, they weren't sure what they ought to do.

My pistol was empty, but they didn't realize that, so I kept it trained on them.

I said tightly, "Take a good look at the man that killed my father. Being a member of the Davis police didn't save his dirty hide; that's something the rest of you might remember."

"Tall," Pat Roark said again. I started backing out, keeping them covered with my empty pistol.

Outside, we hit the saddles and our horses lit out for the far end of the street in one startled jump. The other ranchers fell in behind us, fogging it out of John's City.

We traveled north toward Garner's Store for maybe two miles, and then the ranchers started splitting up, cutting out from the main body and heading toward their own outfits. They were nervous men for the most part, and I could see by their faces that they thought they had been suckered into something that they hadn't bargained for. Well, I thought, to hell with them. If they were afraid to fight for their own kind, there was nothing I could do for them.

By the time we reached the store, Pat Roark was the only one still with me. As we let our horses drink at the trough, Pat stood up in his stirrups, looking back along the road.

"The police don't seem so damned anxious to follow us," he said, still with that thin grin of his.

I wasn't worrying about the police. It was the cavalry that was going to give us trouble when they heard about it. We hitched our horses and went inside the store.

Old Man Garner wasn't glad to see us. Things had a way of happening to people who helped fugitives. A man's store could burn down, or he could get robbed blind. All kinds of things could happen.

He came slowly out of the dark interior of the store. He could smell trouble and he didn't like it.

"Tall, you get out of here," he said gruffly. "I know the police are after you; so don't tell me different."

"I'm not going to tell you different, Mr. Garner. But they won't be along for a while. Is my credit still good?"

He grunted. "I reckon. If it'll get you out of here."

We got a dozen boxes of .44 cartridges, some meal, salt, and a slab of bacon. "If you don't see me for a while," I said, "you can get the money from Ma."

"Money won't do me no good," he said peevishly, "if the police catch me helpin' you out this way. Now scat, both of you." Then on impulse, he went behind the counter and came out with a small tin skillet and a bag of ground coffee. "You might as well take these too, as long as you're gettin' everything else you want."

I took the things and wrapped them up in newspapers. Old Man Garner didn't like turncoats any better than most people, and he wasn't as put out about helping us as he tried to make us believe. As we started back for our horses, I said, "When the bluebellies come along you might just mention that you saw us heading east, toward Indian Ridge."

At last his curiosity got the best of him. "Did you . . . kind of get things settled up, Tall?"

"As well as it can be settled," I said. "Remember, east, toward Indian Ridge."

"I won't forget. Now go on, get out of here."

We headed northwest along the road to the Bannerman ranch for a mile or more, and then cut due west on some hard shale that would be difficult to trail us on. We moved on up to some low rolling hills and finally reached the arroyo. I looked at Pat Roark.

He was a funny guy. And, as we headed toward Daggert's Road, I began to wonder just why he was sticking his neck out this way. The Roarks had a small one-horse outfit over east of John's City — that is, the old man had the outfit. Pat, I remembered, was the youngest of five sons, and the others had drifted off to other parts of Texas before the war and hadn't been heard from since. Pat's old man had never amounted to much. What little money he made by brush popping went mostly for whiskey. Pat had never had the money to attend old Professor Bigloe's academy like the rest of us.

So maybe he was just looking for a chance

to get away from John's City, and he figured this was it. Whatever the reason, I was glad to have him along.

We rode down the arroyo until we came to the cut-away that Ray Novak and I had ducked into before. Pat had never seen the place. I held some of the vines and scrub trees back and motioned him to go on in, and he said, "Well, I'll be damned." He looked around appreciatively as I covered the entrance again. "So this is Daggert's Road," he said. "Well, it'll be nearly hell for anybody to find us in a place like this."

I said, "It'll do for tonight. We'll go on up to the old cabin and stay there. If things look all right I'll ride over to our place. There's that red horse of mine. I sure would hate to leave him behind."

It was clear that we weren't going to be able to stay around John's City for long. Pretty soon the cavalry would be cutting tracks all over northern Texas looking for us, and it wouldn't be the work gang if they caught us this time. It would be a hanging.

Then, for the first time, I thought of those dead men back there in the saloon. I didn't feel anything for them, not even hate, because most of the hate had burned itself out the minute I emptied my pistol. There was just the faint feeling of satisfaction, that kind of feeling that comes to a man after he has paid off a big debt, and that was all. I didn't experience those few hard minutes, the way I had after killing Paul Creyton.

Four men I had killed in as many days — but even that didn't bother me. They had all needed killing. Nobody held it against you for killing a horse thief like Creyton. And Thornton and the other two policemen weren't any different. I would have to hide out for a while, until the carpetbaggers were out of Texas. A year, maybe. Two at the most, because Texans wouldn't stand for that kind of treatment for long. Then I could come back and stand trial. No jury of John's City ranchers would convict me for what I had done.

There were only two things that bothered me. How would Ma get along without me or Pa to look after her? And Laurin — it was going to be a hard year, or two years, being away from her.

"Is that the place?" Pat Roark pointed toward the sagging shack at the end of the trail.

I nodded. "I guess that'll hold us for a few hours. We can fill our bellies and rest our horses, and figure out where to go."

Pat laughed. "While the bluebellies cut tracks all over Indian Ridge."

Nothing seemed to bother him. If he regretted having to pull out like this, without even a chance to say good-by to his old man, it didn't show on that grinning face of his. He seemed to have completely forgotten the fact that he had killed a man a short time back.

We picketed our horses behind the shack where there was plenty of new green grass. By the time we got our saddles off and lugged our supplies inside it was almost dark. I wondered about making a fire, then decided we might as well have a hot meal while we had a chance.

Later, as we sat on the dirt floor eating dripping pieces of bacon and hoecake, Pat said, "I know it's none of my business, and don't get the idea I'm complaining, but don't you think it's a little dangerous staying this close to John's City? We could cover some ground tonight without punishing our horses."

"I told you I didn't want to leave that red horse behind," I said. "Hell, the cavalry won't find us here. They'll be cutting tracks on Indian Ridge, like you said."

Pat shrugged. "All right. I was just thinking."

Probably he knew the real reason I didn't want to pull out right away. It was Laurin, not that red horse. But he didn't say any more about it.

As night came on, we put the fire out, and my ears seemed to grow sharper as darkness closed in. The moan of the wind and the rattle of grass made startling sounds in the night. Once I got up abruptly and went outside with my gun in my hand when I heard a movement in the brush. But it turned out to be a swamp rabbit making his bed for the night under a clump of mesquite.

Pat said, "You'd better go see about that horse, if you're so almighty anxious about him."

He didn't say I was getting the jumps, but that was what he meant. All the things that had happened today began to grow and magnify in the darkness. I wouldn't let myself think about Pa. I had done all I could. He would understand that, wherever he was.

But Laurin was something else. She hadn't wanted me to go to town in the first place. What was she going to say about those blue-bellies that I hoped were burning in hell by now? Somehow, I had to explain that to her before I went away. And I wasn't sure how I was going to do it.

I said, "Maybe you're right, Pat. I'll see

about the horse. Then maybe we'll cover some ground before daybreak."

"Whatever you say." He had torn off a piece of his shirttail and was using it to clean that new .44 I had given him.

"You'll be all right here," I said. "The cavalry won't get around tonight."

"Don't worry about me." He looked up. "You're the one that better watch out the bluebellies don't get you."

It was completely dark now. I went outside and got the bay saddled, and Pat came to the door and watched as I rode off.

It wasn't a smart thing to do, I knew that. Pappy Garret would have skinned me alive for pulling a fool stunt like that . . . but it was one of those things that I had to see all the way through. Before long — if I didn't set things straight with Laurin — I'd be snapping at Pat, and we'd end up the same as me and Ray Novak, riding our own separate trails. And I needed Pat. One man wasn't any good on the run. Pappy had been proof of that. It occurred to me that I had already learned to think the way Pappy Garret thought. I didn't really give a damn for Pat Roark, but I could use him, and that was what I meant to do.

That shocked me for a moment. A few days ago I had never even thought of killing a man, and now I had four to my credit, a longer string than a lot of well-known bad-men could boast. I felt nothing for them. They could have been calf-killing coyotes, and not human beings.

I tried to work back in my mind and find the beginning of it. Paul Creyton — there was nothing I could have done about that. He had been trying to steal my horse, and that was reason enough for killing anybody in this country. And Thornton — nobody could blame me for that. And the other two — they had been pulling on me, and if I hadn't killed them they would have killed me. I hadn't started any of it. They had all brought it on themselves.

But still I could taste the uneasy tang of doubt, and I wondered if it all would seem so clear-cut and inevitable to Laurin as it did to me.

Coming out of the hills, I rode straight east, heading for our place. I would have a hard time explaining it to Pat, if I came back without that red horse, and, besides, for some strange reason, I wanted to put off seeing Laurin until the very last.

There was no sign of cavalry or police as I crossed the open range. Probably, I thought, the Cameron ranch would be the last place they would look for me, especially if Old

Man Garner had told them we were headed for Indian Ridge.

The ranch house was dark when I got there. The only light I could see was in the bunkhouse. When we reached the rear of the ranch yard, I got down and led the bay toward the barn where I figured Red would be.

"Tall."

It was just a whisper, but there in the darkness it came at me like a bullet. I dropped the reins and wheeled.

"It's me, Tall! My God, be careful with that gun!"

It was Bucky Stow, coming from the far side of the barn. I didn't remember pulling my pistol, but there it was, in my hand, the hammer pulled back and ready to fall. I heard somebody breathing hard, breath whistling through his teeth. After a moment I realized it was me.

"You want to be careful how you slip up on people," I said weakly. Bucky would never know how close he came to being number five on my string. I shoved the pistol back in my holster.

"Tall, what in hell are you doin' here, anyway? There's cavalry and police all over this part of Texas."

"I came after that red horse," I said. "Is

he ready to go?"

Bucky screwed up his face. "I reckon," he said. "But he could stand fattening up. A horse like Red ain't supposed to take that kind of treatment."

"Never mind about Red, he can take it. Is Ma doing all right?"

"She's over at the Novak place now," he said, rubbing his chin sadly. "She kind of figured that maybe you'd come back here. She wanted me to tell you to come to Virginia as soon as you get a chance."

I looked at him. "Virginia?"

"She's selling the ranch and moving back there with her people. Runnin' a ranch is too big a job for a woman. And since your pa . . ."

His voice trailed off, but I knew what he was thinking. Now that Pa was gone, and I couldn't stay here to help her, there was nothing else for her to do. It hurt me at first, thinking about giving up this ranch that Pa had worked so hard for. But Ma had never really liked it. She only wanted to be where Pa was. It was the best thing, I thought, for her to move back with her own people until I could clear myself with the Texas courts.

I said, "Tell her I'm all right, Bucky. Tell her not to worry about me, and I'll see her in Virginia as soon as this thing blows over."

Bucky said, "Sure, Tall. Now I'll get that horse for you."

He went in the barn and in a few minutes he came back with Red, all saddled and ready to go. I slapped the horse's glossy rump. "You ready to travel, boy? You got your belly full of corn?"

Red switched his head around and nuzzled the front of my shirt. I thought wryly, That's the first sincere gesture of welcome I've had since I got back.

CHAPTER 6

I didn't try to go to the Novaks' and say good-by to Ma. That would be pushing my luck too far. I got on Red and we headed west again, crossing the Bannerman wagon road just in case the cavalry was up in that direction, then we went north, cross-country, until the big ranch house and barns loomed up in the darkness. I didn't have any guarantee that there weren't any soldiers in one of those barns just waiting for me to pull a fool stunt like this, but that was a chance I had to take. As I got closer, I saw that there was a light in the back of the house, in the kitchen.

I left Red at the side of the house, and the back door opened.

"Joe, is that you?"

Then I stepped into the light, and Laurin gasped. Her hands and arms were white with flour, and there was a pale powdery smudge on the side of her nose. She was just beginning to bake the week's supply of bread.

"Tall!" Her voice was frightened. "Tall, you can't come here. The cavalry left only an hour ago, looking for you."

"The cavalry can't keep me away from you," I said. "Nothing can."

Quickly, she dusted her hands and arms on her apron and came down the steps. I put my hands on her shoulders and I could feel her shiver as I drew her close and held her tight. "Oh, Tall," she cried, "it's no good. Meeting this way, in darkness, afraid to be seen together."

I kissed her lightly and we stood there clinging to each other. I pressed her head to my shoulder and the clean smell of her hair worked on me like fever. "I'll come back," I said. "It won't always be like this." Then I asked the question that I was half afraid to ask. "Laurin, will you wait for me? Will you trust me to straighten things out in my own way?"

For a moment she didn't say anything. Her body was rigid against me and I knew that she was crying.

"You know I'll wait," she said at last. "Forever, I suppose, if I have to. It's just that I'm afraid . . . something awful and wrong is happening to us."

I knew she was thinking about those three men. . . . She didn't know about the fourth. "Can't you see, I had to do it?" I said. "I couldn't just stand by and let them get away with it — doing what they did. You see that, don't you?"

"I don't know," she breathed. "I just don't know."

"I'm not going to get into any more trouble," I said. "Don't be afraid of that. I'll join a trail herd and go up to Kansas until the bluebellies are out of Texas courts. Then I'll come back and stand trial."

She raised her head and looked at me for a long time. And at last she began to believe it.

"I'll wait," she said quietly. "If you'll do that, I'll wait as long as I need to. It won't be too long."

That was the way I remembered her, the way she looked as she said, "I'll wait." And then her face softened, and for a moment it seemed that she was almost happy. "I'll get you some bacon," she said, "and some fresh bread. You'll need something to eat while you're traveling."

"We'll get supplies," I said. I didn't want to go, but the time had come and I couldn't put it off any longer. Then I kissed her — hard enough to last as long as it had to last.

"Don't you worry," I said. "I'll come back."
It seemed that I was saying that more often
than was necessary to convince her. Maybe
I was trying to convince myself.

I looked back once as I rode away, and
she was still standing there with the lamplight streaming out the door and falling over
her like a veil of fine silk. She half lifted her
hand, as if to wave, and then let it drop.
After a while, she went back into the house
and that was the last I saw of her.

It was a quiet trip riding back to the shack.
There was no sign of soldiers or police
anywhere, and I made up my mind to get
out of this part of Texas as soon as I got
back to where Pat Roark was. I was afraid
that we had stretched our luck about as far
as it would go.

I judged that it was about midnight by the
time we reached the hills. I nudged Red
down into the gully that was Daggert's
Road and stopped for a moment to listen,
but there was still no sound except the faint
night wind and the faraway bark of a coyote.
We had almost reached the cabin when Red
started shying away from something in the
darkness.

I pulled up again and listened. There still
wasn't anything that I could see or hear,
but that didn't mean that there was nothing

out there in the darkness. I felt of Red's ears. They were pricked up, stiff, his head cocked to one side. I reached far over and felt of his muzzle. It was hot and dry.

That worried me. Normally a horse's nose is cool and moist; it's only when he senses danger that it gets that hot, dry feel. Then I felt little ripples of nervousness in the long muscles of his neck. I knew something was wrong. But before I could do anything about it, a voice shouted:

"Throw up your hands, Cameron. We've got you surrounded!"

Instinctively, I drove the steel in Red's ribs and he jumped forward with a startled snort. I didn't know who was doing the shouting, but I could guess. I dumped out of the saddle as we neared the cabin, and Red spurted on like a scared ghost, heading for higher ground. I hit the ground hard, rolled, and scrambled for the door of the shack. If I had stayed on Red, they would have cut me down before he could have taken a dozen jumps, and besides, that gully of a road led to a dead end about a hundred rods up in the hills.

A rifle bellowed in the darkness, another one answered it, and then the whole night seemed to explode to life. Carbines, I thought as I crawled the last few yards to the doorway on my hands and knees. Cavalry carbines. Why the hell doesn't Pat shoot back?

Then my foot hit something soft and wet and sticky, and I had my answer. Pat Roark was dead. I didn't have to make an inspection to know that. I tried hurriedly to roll him over and it was like rolling a limp sack of wet grain. I let him stay where he was, got the door closed, and fumbled in the darkness for the window.

The shooting had stopped now. They saw that they had missed me on the first try, and now they were ready to think up something else. I wondered why they hadn't placed a man in the shack to shoot me as I came in — but I got my answer to that, too, as I was fumbling around looking for an extra box of cartridges. There *was* a man in here.

But he was dead, the same as Pat. The hard-visored forage cap on the floor told me that he was a soldier, probably a cavalryman. I felt for his head and jerked my hand back as I touched the clammy sticky mess that had leaked out of the hole in his skull. Well, they had done a good job on each other, I thought grimly.

I went back to the window and tried to see something. They hadn't started to move in yet. Probably, they were in positions on high ground overlooking the cabin, but I hadn't had time to notice that much when the shooting was going on. There was a little clearing all around the shack and I could watch three sides from the windows and door. But the rear was blind.

I took another look to make sure that they hadn't decided to rush me, then I went to the rear wall and began to knock out the 'dobe plaster between the logs. In a minute I had a porthole cleaned out big enough to shoot through and see through. But I wasn't sure how much good that was going to do me. I couldn't be in four places at once.

"Come out with your hands up, Cameron," the same voice shouted, "and we'll see you get a fair trial in court!"

I could imagine what kind of a trial I'd get in a carpetbag court, after killing three state policemen. I went back to the west window and looked out carefully. The voice, I judged, was coming from behind a rock up above the gully. An officer, probably.

"This is your last chance, Cameron!"

"Go to hell," I shouted. "If you want me, come and get me."

Nothing happened, and I began to wonder what they were waiting on. They had me surrounded. I wasn't questioning their word about that. Then why didn't they close in and begin shooting me to pieces? That's what I would have done if I had been in their place. Or maybe burn the cabin down. That would make a clean job of it.

But they were still waiting on something. I felt my way across the shack again and got my other pistol out of Pat Roark's dead hand. I rolled the soldier over against the wall to get him out of the way, and, as I was giving him the last nudge with, my boot, the answer came to me.

The reason they were reluctant to start any wild shooting or burning was that they thought their man was still alive. I went back and inspected Pat Roark a little closer this time. Sure enough, he was still warm, lying there in the doorway with a bullet in his gut. It all began to make sense now. I could almost see it, the way it must have worked.

Pat had been out of the cabin for some reason when the ambush had been set, and when he came back, there was the soldier waiting to take him. I could imagine the way Pat Roark's face must have looked. He probably never even lost his grin as he jerked that .44 and shot the trooper's brains out. But not before he got a carbine slug in the gut for his trouble.

The others must have been wondering where I was and had set themselves to catch me when I came back — if I came back. Anyway, there was the dead cavalryman, and Pat, who must have lived two or three hours with a hot lead slug in his belly, waiting for me to come back and save him. But I hadn't got back in time. And I couldn't have saved him anyway. I couldn't even save myself now.

The best I could do was to try to keep things going the way Pat had started it, by making the cavalry believe that their man was still alive.

"All right," the voice behind the rock called. "We gave you your chance, Cameron. Now, we're coming after you."

I shouted, "Try it and this trooper of yours gets a bullet in his brain."

I had guessed right. That had them worried.

"How do we know he's not already dead?" the voice wanted to know.

"Why don't you come in and see for yourself?"

But they didn't accept the invitation. They were going to think it over a while longer, and in the meantime I had some time for thinking myself. I wondered how they found this shack so quick. Probably some turncoat had told them about it. I kept forgetting that Texas was full of traitors. I remembered Pappy Garret saying once, "One mistake is all a man is allowed when he's on the run." It looked like I had made mine early.

I kept moving from window to window, from the door to the rear of the shack, but I still couldn't see anything to shoot at. The waiting began to get on my nerves. I couldn't very well make a deal with them. I couldn't get away without a horse, and from the way Red was going the last time I saw him I guessed he must be close to Kansas by now.

So we waited some more. From time to time the voice would yell for me to come out or they were coming after me. But they kept holding off. Then, as the first pale light began to show in the east, I knew they had finally made up their minds. I could hear them moving around out there, and the officer giving orders in a low, hushed voice. They had decided their man was dead. There was no use for them to wait any longer.

I could hear them spreading out, circling the cabin. It was light enough to see by now, but they were behind rocks or brush, waiting for the signal to rush. I waited by the west window, thinking, So this is the way it's going to end — when the shooting and yelling started at the rear of the cabin. I jumped over to the rear wall and got a pistol through the crack. I shot twice before I saw that there was nothing to shoot at.

It was a trick. They had planted two or three men back there to draw my attention while the others started rushing from the front and two sides. I wheeled and headed back for one of the windows, but I could already see that it was too late. They were almost on me before I could get a shot off. I remember thinking coolly all the time, I'll have time to get one of them, maybe two. They'll have to pay for me if they get me. And I fired point blank into a cavalryman's face. The man running beside him fell away to one side, hit the ground and scrambled for the cabin. Behind me, I heard the others closing in on my blind sides.

I wheeled away from the window and took a shot out of the door. Then I saw a crazy thing. One of them stumbled, grabbed his belly and fell — not the one I was shooting at, but another one. Then I saw another one fall, and another one.

I didn't try to understand what was happening. For a moment I stood there dumb with surprise, and, by that time, panic had taken hold of the cavalry and they scrambled

154

again for cover, what was left of them. I circled the inside of the cabin, counting the soldiers that hadn't made it back to cover. There were six of them. That stunned me. I had accounted for only one of them. I was sure of that. Then who had killed the other five?

Probably the cavalry was wondering the same thing. I could hear the officer shouting angrily, trying to get his men grouped for another rush. And after a minute they came again. Their force was cut to half this time, but they came running and yelling from all sides. Before I could raise my pistols, one went down. Then another one.

I didn't even bother to shoot again. The cavalry had had enough. They turned and scattered like scared rabbits, and there wasn't any officer to pull them together this time. The officer, a lieutenant, lay outside my window with a rifle bullet in his brain.

It had happened too fast to try to understand it. I only knew that there were eight dead men outside the shack, and I had killed only one of them. I heard the cavalry detail — what was left of it — scrambling down in the gully, and pretty soon there was the clatter of hoofs and the rattle of chain and metal as they lit out for the south. By this time they probably figured that the

155

cabin was haunted, that there was a devil in there instead of an eighteen-year-old kid. And I wasn't so sure that they were so far wrong.

I should have known, I suppose, with that kind of shooting — but Pappy Garret never entered my mind until I saw him coming down from the high ground, astride that big black horse with the white diamond in the center of its forehead. He was riding slouched in the saddle, looking more like a circuit-riding preacher than anything else, except for that deadly new rifle, still cradled in the crook of his arm. In one hand he held a pair of reins, and that big red horse of mine was coming along behind.

Pappy rode up in the clearing in front of the cabin, looking at me mildly, with that half-grin of his. Then he snapped the leaf sight down on his rifle, and sighed. Like a woodsman putting away his ax after a good day's work.

"Son," he said soberly, "you sure as hell have got a lot to learn."

"Where did you come from?" I blurted. "How did you know I was here?"

"Now don't start asking a lot of damnfool questions," he said. "You'd better just climb on this horse, because we've got ourselves some hard riding to do."

It was incredible that Pappy would stick his neck out like this to help a kid like me. But there he was. And if I wanted to be smart, I'd just be thankful and let it go at that.

I managed to say, "Thanks, Pappy. If you ever need a favor . . . well, I owe you one."

I went in the cabin and gathered up the extra cartridges and grub and rolled it all up in a blanket. In a few minutes I had it all tied behind the saddle and was ready to go.

Pappy looked at me, and then at Red. He said, "We'll see now if that red horse was worth killing for." Then he added, "He'd better be."

For the next four days, I learned what hard riding really was. Pappy had it worked out to a science. Walk, canter, gallop. Walk, canter, gallop. Rest your horse five minutes every hour. Water him every chance you got, but be careful not to let him have too much at once. Steal grain for him. Raid cornfields or homestead barns. Take wild chances — chances that a man wouldn't dare take for money — just to get a few ears of corn for your horse.

We didn't have time to eat, ourselves. The horses were the important things. I wanted to stop and cook some bacon, but Pappy said no. He had some jerky that he saved for times like this, so we chewed that while we rode. We traveled cross-country, never touching the stage roads except to cross them. Skirting all towns and settlements. Avoiding communities where we saw telegraph wires strung up.

Then, on the fourth day, we saw red dust boiling up ahead of us like low-hanging clouds. And as we got closer we could hear the bawling of cattle and the hoarse cursing of trail hands. At last we pulled up on a small rise and looked down on the constant stream of animals and men. It didn't look like an easy way to get to Kansas, but it was the best way for us. The law didn't bother trail herds. The big ranchers and cattle buyers saw to that. Their job was to get cattle to the railheads in Kansas, and they weren't particular about the men they hired, as long as they got the job done.

"Well, Pappy?" I said.

Pappy shook his head. "This is still dangerous country. Probably those cattle were gathered around Uvalde. They'll travel along the eastern line of army posts until they get to Red River Station. We'll push on east and catch a herd coming up the Brazos."

So we headed east and north, skirting the main trails until we got to Red River Station. The Station was a wild, restless place, milling with bawling cattle, and wild-eyed trail bosses trying to keep their herds in check until their time came to make the crossing. Herds from all over Texas gathered here to make their push through Indian Territory — shaggy brush cattle from along the Nueces, as wild and murderous as grizzlies; scrawny, hungry-looking steers all the way from Christi; fat, well-fed ones from the Brazos. Wild cattle and the near-wild men that drove them, all took advantage of the Station's limited facilites to break the monotonous, fatiguing routine of trail life.

The only building there was a long, cigar-box-shaped log hut along the river bank, and Pappy and I made for it. There was no sign of police or cavalry, and, when I mentioned it to Pappy, he laughed dryly.

"They wouldn't do any good here. In the first place, it would take a regiment of cavalry and the whole damn state police force to make an impression on a bunch of drovers. Anyway, all a man has to do is jump across the river and he's in Indian Territory where the police couldn't follow him."

There was a long bar inside the Station's one building, where men stood two deep waiting for their wildcat whiskey at two bits a drink. There was gambling in the back of

the place, and half-breed saloon girls moving among the customers, promoting one
kind of deal or another. Pappy and I waited
at the bar until the bartender got around to
us.

"Well, son, what do you think of it?"

"I'm not sure," I said. "I never saw anything like it before."

Pappy grinned slightly. "Wait until you see
Abilene." He picked up a bottle and we
went to a table in the back of the place. It
felt good to sit down in a chair for a change,
instead of a saddle. I didn't feel sleepy. You
got the idea that nobody ever slept in a
place like this. There was too much excitement for that.

I said, "Do you think we'll be safe here?"

"As safe as we'd be anywhere," Pappy
said. "As long as we don't overdo it. I'll look
around and pick out a herd to hook up with
before long. Abilene beats this place. Besides, the marshal there is a friend of mine."

For the past four days, I hadn't had time
to think. And now I was too tired to think.
The fight with the cavalry seemed a long
way in the past. It was hard to believe that
it had happened.

We stayed at Red River Station that night,
spreading our blanket rolls on the ground,
the way the drovers did, and the next day

Pappy went to see about a job for us.

That was the day I met Bat Steuber, a wiry little remuda man from an outfit down on the Brazos. A remuda man, I figured, might be able to rustle up some grain for Red and that big black of Pappy's, if he was handled right.

The way to handle him, it turned out, was with whiskey. I bought him three drinks of wildcat with Pappy's money and he couldn't do enough for me. He took me down to where the outfit was camped and got some shelled corn out of the forage wagon. Or rather, he was about to get the corn, when a man came up behind the wagon and cut it short.

"The boss says look after the horses," the man said.

He was a big man, his shoulders and chest bulging his faded blue shirt. His eyes were red-rimmed from riding long days in the drag, and his mouth was tight, looking as if he hadn't smiled for a long time.

Bat Steuber said, "Hell, Buck, I finished my shift. It's your . . ."

The man cut him off again. "I said see about the horses."

The voice cracked and Steuber jumped to his feet. "Sure, Buck, if you say so."

The man watched vacantly as Steuber

went back to the rear where the remuda was ringed in; then he turned to me. I had a crazy idea that I had seen the man before, but at the same time I knew I hadn't. There was something about him that was familiar. His eyes maybe. I had seen eyes like those somewhere, clear, and blue, and deadly. He wore matched .44's converted, the same as mine, and I didn't have to be told that he knew how to use them. There are some things you know without having it proved to you.

"What's your name, kid?" he asked flatly.

"Cameron," I said. "Talbert Cameron. I don't think I caught yours."

He looked as if he hadn't heard me. "You're the kid that rode in with Pappy Garret yesterday, ain't you?"

He was asking a lot of questions, in a country where it wasn't polite to ask a stranger too many questions.

But I said, "That's right."

I thought something happened to those eyes of his. He said flatly, "When you see Pappy, tell him I'm looking for him to kill him."

For a moment, I just stood there with my back against the wagon wheel. He said it so quietly and matter-of-factly that you wondered afterward if he had spoken at all.

I tried to keep my voice as level as his. "Don't you think that'll be kind of a job? Men have tried it before, I hear."

His voice took an edge. "You just tell him what I said, kid. That way maybe you'll live to be a man someday." He turned abruptly and started to walk away. Then he turned again. "Just tell him Buck Creyton is ready any time he wants to show his guts. If there is any question as to why I want to kill him, you might ask if he remembers my brother Paul."

He was gone before I could think of anything to say. Buck Creyton — a name as deadly as a soft-nosed bullet. A name as well known as Pappy Garret's, when the talk got around to gun-fighters.

I thought, Have you lost your guts? Why didn't you tell him that you were the one that killed his brother, and not Pappy?

I didn't know. I just thought of those deadly blue eyes and felt my insides turn over. He would kill me without batting an eye. Then I thought, Just like I killed his brother, and the three policemen, and the cavalryman.

I walked over to Red and swung up to the saddle. "Come on, boy," I said. "Let's get out of here."

CHAPTER 7

I waited for Pappy at the camp we had made, up the river from the herds. I wasn't sure whether I wanted to run or to stay with Pappy and see the thing through with Creyton. Maybe I would have the decision made for me, if Pappy ran into Creyton before he got back to camp.

Then — out of nowhere — I heard the words: Don't worry about me. I'm not going to get into any more trouble. They sounded well worn and bitter. They were words I had said to Laurin, and a few hours later I had killed another man, a soldier.

Now I had the government officers on my tail as well as the state police. Laurin . . . I'd hardly had time to think about her until now. I could close my eyes and see her. I could almost touch her. But not quite.

I picked up a rock and flung it viciously out of sheer helplessness and anger.

I hadn't asked to get into trouble. It was

like playing a house game with the deck stacked against you. The longer you played, the harder you tried to get even, and the more you lost. Where would it stop? Could it be stopped at all?

I realized what I was doing, and changed my thinking. You'd go crazy thinking that way. Or lose your guts maybe, and get yourself killed. And I wasn't planning on getting killed, by Buck Creyton, or the police, or anybody else. I had to keep living and get back to John's City. I had to get back to Laurin.

They didn't really have anything against me — except, of course, that one trooper that I had shot up at Daggert's cabin. But a jury of ranchers wouldn't hang me for shooting a bluebelly. Just lay quiet, I told myself, and wait for the right time.

But there was still Buck Creyton to think about. My mind kept coming back to him. I wondered vaguely if Paul Creyton had any more kinfolks that would be bent on avenging him. Or the policemen, or the trooper.

At last, when I finally went back to the beginning of the trouble, there was Ray Novak. He was the one who had started it all. I realized then that I hated Ray Novak more than anybody else, and sooner or later . . .

But caution tugged again in the back of my mind. Lie quiet, it said. Don't ask for more trouble.

Pappy came in a little before sundown, covered with trail dust and looking dog tired. I didn't know how to break it to him about Buck Creyton. I wasn't sure what he would do when he found out that Creyton was after him for something he hadn't done.

"I got us fixed up with a job of work," he said, wetting his bandanna from his saddle canteen and wiping it over his dirty face. "The Box-A outfit needs a pair of swing riders to see them through the Territory. Forty dollars a month if we use our own horses. That all right with you?"

"I guess so," I said.

He wrung his bandanna out and tied it around his neck again. "You don't sound very proud of it," he said. But he grinned as he said it. I could see that Pappy was in good spirits. "It seemed like I rode halfway to the Rio Grande looking for that outfit," he went on. "But it's what we want. The trail boss is a friend of mine and he don't allow anybody to cut his help for strays. Cavalry included." He patted his belly. "Say, is there any of that bacon left?"

"Sure," I said. I got the slab and cut it up while Pappy made the fire. I decided I'd better let him eat first before saying anything.

It was almost dark by the time we finished eating. Pappy sat under a cottonwood as I wiped the skillet, staring mildly across the wide, sandy stretch of land that was Red River. There was almost no river to it, just a little stream in the middle of that wide, dusty bed. Quicksand, not water, was what made it dangerous to cross.

I put the skillet with the blanket roll and decided that now was as good a time as any.

"Pappy," I said abruptly, "we're in trouble."

He made one of those sounds of his that passed for laughter. "We *were* in trouble," he said, "Not any more. We've got clear sailing now, all the way to Kansas."

"I don't mean with the police. With Buck Creyton."

I saw him stiffen for a moment. Slowly, he began to relax. "Just what do you mean by that?" he asked. Some people, when they get suddenly mad, they yell, or curse, or maybe hit the closest thing they can find. But not Pappy. His voice took on a soft, velvety quality, almost like the purring of a big cat. That's the way his voice was now.

But I had gone too far to back down. I said, "I saw him today. He's working with one of the outfits getting ready to make the crossing. He's looking for you, Pappy. He says he's going to kill you."

Pappy sat very still. Then he said, "You yellow little bastard."

The words hit like a slap in the face. I wheeled on him, my hands about to jump for my guns, but then I remembered what Pappy had done to Ray Novak, and dropped them to my side.

"Look, Pappy," I said tightly, "you've got this figured all wrong."

He didn't even hear me. "You told him I was the one that killed Paul, didn't you?"

"I didn't tell him a thing," I said.

"I'll bet! You didn't tell him that *you* did it." Slowly he got to his feet, his hands never moving more than an inch or so from the butts of his pistols.

I suppose I was scared at first, but, surprisingly, that went away. I began to breathe normally again. If he was determined to think that I had crossed him, there was nothing I could do about it. If he was determined to force a shoot-out, there was nothing I could do about that, either. He was standing in a half crouch, like a lean, hungry cat about to spring.

"You yellow little bastard," he said again.

I said, "Don't say that any more, Pappy.

I'm warning you, don't use that word again."

I think that surprised him. He thought I was afraid of him, and now it kind of jarred him to find out I wasn't. Pappy was good with a gun. I'd seen him draw and I knew. Maybe he was better than me — a hundred times better, maybe — but he hadn't proved it yet.

He said, "I picked you up. I went to the trouble to save your lousy hide, and this is what I get. This tears it wide open, son. This finishes us."

"If you're not going to listen to reason," I said, "then go ahead and make your move. You've got a big name as a gun-slinger. Let's see how good you really are."

He laughed silently. "I wouldn't want to take advantage of a kid."

I was mad now. He hadn't given me a chance to explain because he thought he could ride his reputation over me. I said, "Don't worry about the advantage. If you think you've got me scared, if you think I'm going to beg out of a shooting, then you're crazy as hell."

He still didn't move. "You think you're something, don't you, son? Because you got lucky with Paul Creyton, because you killed a couple of state policemen who didn't rightly know which end of a gun to hold, you think you're a gunman. You've got a lot to learn, son."

"Draw, then," I almost shouted. "If you think you're so goddamned good and I'm so bad. Draw and get it over with. You're the one that got your back up."

For a moment I thought he was going to do it. I could see the smoky haze of anger lying far back in those pale eyes of his. I felt muscles and nerves tightening in my arms and shoulders, waiting for Pappy to make a move.

Suddenly he began to relax. The haze went out of his eyes and he sat slowly down by the cottonwood.

"What the hell got into us anyway?" he asked, shaking his head in amazement. "Hell, I don't want to kill you. I don't think you want to kill me. Sit down, son, until the heat wears off."

It took me a long time to relax, but I didn't feel very big because I had made Pappy Garret back down. I knew it wasn't because he was afraid of me.

"Go on," Pappy said softly, "sit down and let's think this thing over."

The anger that had been burning so hot only a minute ago had now burned itself out. Me and Pappy getting ready to kill each other — the thought of that left me cold and empty. Pappy had saved my life, he had given me a chance to live so someday I could go back to Laurin.

"It's just as well we got that out of our systems," Pappy said at last. "I'm sorry about the things I said. I didn't mean them."

That was probably the first time Pappy had ever apologized to anybody for anything. And he was right. It was just as well that we got it out of our systems. Sooner or later, when two men live by their guns, they are bound to come together. But there was slight chance of it happening again. You don't usually buck a man if you know he isn't afraid of you.

Pappy got out his tobacco and corn-shuck papers, giving all his attention to building a cigarette. After he had finished, he tossed the makings to me.

I said, "Hell, I guess I was just hot-headed, Pappy. I'm ready to forget it if you are. We're too good a team to break up by shooting each other."

Then Pappy smiled — that complete, face-splitting smile that he used so seldom. "Forgotten," he said.

After it was all over, I felt closer to Pappy than I had ever felt before. We sat for a good while, as darkness came on, smoking those corn-shuck cigarettes of his, and not saying anything. But I guess we both had Buck Creyton in our minds. I had already decided that I would hunt Creyton down the next day and tell him just the way it happened; then if he was still set on killing somebody, he could try it on me. I couldn't guess what Pappy was thinking until he said:

"This is as good a time as any to push across the river. You get that red horse of yours, son, and we'll be moving as soon as it's a little darker."

I got the wrong idea at first. I thought Pappy was running because he was afraid of a shoot-out with Buck Creyton. But then I realized that he wouldn't admit it that way if he was. At least he would make up some kind of excuse for pulling out.

But he didn't say anything, and then I began to get it. He was moving out on my account. He was ready to cross the Territory without the protection of a trail herd so that Buck Creyton wouldn't have a chance to find out that I was the one who had killed his brother. He was protecting me, not himself.

I didn't see the sense in it. It seemed like it was just putting off a fight that was bound to come sooner or later, and why not get it over with now? But I didn't want to argue. I didn't want another flare-up with Pappy like I'd just had. So I went after Red.

We crossed the river about a mile above the Station, keeping well east of the main trail, and pushed into Indian Territory. We rode without saying anything much. I didn't know how Pappy felt about it, but I didn't like the idea of running away from a fight that was bound to come sometime anyway. I figured he must have his reasons, so I let him have his way.

By daybreak, Pappy said we were almost to the Washita, and it was as good a place as any to pitch camp. The next day we pushed on across the Canadian, into some low, rolling hills, and that was where I began to see Pappy's reason for running.

First, we picked a place to camp near a dry creek bed; then Pappy insisted on scouting the surrounding country before telling me what he had in mind. Fort Gibson was on our right, Pappy said, over on the Arkansas line, but he didn't think it was close enough to bother us. The Fort Sill Indian Reservation was on our left, on the other side of the cattle trail, but the soldiers there were busy with the Indians and wouldn't be looking for us. The thing we had to worry about now, he went on, was government

173

marshals making raids out of the Arkansas country. But we would have to take our chances with them.

"I've told you before," Pappy said, "that you've got a lot to learn." He led the way down to the dry creek bed and pointed to a log about forty yards down from us. "Pull as fast as you can and see how many bullets you can put in it."

It sounded foolish to me. And dangerous. What if soldiers heard the shooting? But I looked at Pappy, and his face was set and dead serious. I shrugged. "All right, if you say so."

I jerked at my righthand gun, but before I could clear leather the morning came to life with one explosion crowding on top of another. Pappy had emptied his own pistols into the log before I had started to shoot.

Pappy looked at me mildly and began punching the empties out of his two .44's. I didn't even bother to draw my own guns. My insides turned over and got cold as I thought of what Pappy could have done to me the other night, if he had wanted to. I breathed deeply a few times before I tried to speak.

At last I said, "All right, Pappy. Where do I start to learn?"

He grinned faintly. "With the holsters

first," he said. "If you don't get your pistols out of your holsters, it doesn't make a damn how good a shot you are." He made me unbuckle my cartridge belts and he examined the leather carefully. "See here?" he said, working one of the .44's gently in and out of the holster. "It binds near the top where it's looped on the belt."

We went up to where the blanket rolls were, and Pappy got some saddle soap out of his bags. "You don't develop a fast draw all at once," he said, rubbing the saddle soap into the leather with his hands. "You cut away a piece of a second here, a piece of a second there, until you've got rid of every bit of motion and friction that's not absolutely necessary. All men aren't made to draw alike. Some like a cross-arm draw, or a waistband draw. Or a shoulder holster under the arm is the best for some men. You've got to find out what comes easiest and then work on it until it's perfect."

He stood back for a moment, looking at me as if I was a horse that he had just bought and he wasn't sure yet what kind of a deal he'd got.

Finally he shook his head. "Your arms are too long for the cross-arm or border draw. That goes the same for the waistband. At the side is the best place, low on your thighs, where your hands cup near the butts when you stand natural. You can't work out any certain way to stand, you've got to be able to shoot from any position."

He handed the belts and holsters back and I buckled them on again like he said. He looked at me critically.

"Unload your pistols and try drawing."

I punched the live rounds out and shoved the guns back in my holsters. Then I grabbed for them and snapped a few times at a spot in front of me.

"Again," Pappy said.

I did it all over again, but Pappy wasn't satisfied. He went over to where his saddle rig was and cut a pair of narrow leather thongs from his own bridle reins. Then he made me stand still, with my legs apart, while he put the thongs through the bottom of my holsters and tied them down to my thighs. "Arms too long, that makes the holsters too low," he said briefly. "They'll flap when you walk if you don't tie them down. Now try it again."

I pulled two more times and snapped on empty chambers so Pappy could get the right perspective.

"I guess they'll do," he said reluctantly. "Now we'll get to the shooting. The drawing can come later."

The dozen boxes of cartridges that I'd got from Old Man Garner went that afternoon. And most of Pappy's extra ammunition went the next day.

"Hell, no!" Pappy would shout when I tried to shoot from the hip. "Aim. That's the reason they put front and rear sights on a pistol, to aim with."

Then I would try it again, holding the pistol straight in front of me, like a girl, aiming and shooting at whatever target Pappy happened to pick. Once in a while Pappy would nod. Once in a great while he would grunt his approval.

"Now aim without drawing your gun," Pappy said finally. "Imagine that you've got your pistol out in front of you, aiming carefully over the sights!" He threw an empty cartridge box about thirty yards down the draw. "Aim at that," he said.

I stood with my arms at my sides, trying to imagine that I was aiming at the box.

"Now draw your pistol and fire. One time. Slow."

I drew and fired, surprised to see the box jump crazily as the bullet slammed into it.

"Now with the other hand," Pappy said.

I tried it again with the left hand and the box jumped again.

I turned around and Pappy was looking at

me strangely. "That'll do for today," he said. He rubbed the ragged beard on his chin, glaring down the draw at the cartridge box. "You've still got a lot to learn," he said gruffly, "but I guess you'll do. It took me two years to learn to shoot like that."

I thought I had been doing something big when, as a kid, I had managed to put a bullet in a tossed-up tin can. But I knew that hadn't been shooting. Not shooting as an exact, deadly science, the way Pappy had worked it out.

The next day we worked on my draw, starting with empty pistols, drawing in carefully studied movements. It was agonizingly slow at first. Arms, and hands, and position of the body had to be correct to the hundredth of an inch. Only after everything was as perfect as it could possibly be did Pappy let me try for speed.

I watched Pappy do it slowly and it seemed so easy. His hands cupping around the butts, starting the upward pull. Thumbs bringing the hammers back as the pistols began to slide out of the holsters, forefingers slipping into the trigger guard. Then firing both pistols, not at the same time, as it seemed, but working in rhythm, taking the kick on one side and then on the other.

"All right, try it," Pappy said.

He pitched out another cartridge box, and I drew slowly, carefully, for the first few times to get the feel of it. Then, as I holstered the pistols again, Pappy shouted:

"Hit it!"

I wheeled instinctively, catching a glimpse of the small cardboard box that Pappy had tossed in the air. The pistols seemed to jump in my hands. The right one roared. Then the left one crowded on top of it. The cartridge box jerked crazily in the air, then fluttered in pieces to the ground.

I stood panting as the last piece of ragged cardboard hit the earth. I could feel myself grinning. I thought, Ray Novak and his two bullets in a tin can! I wondered what Ray Novak would say to shooting like this. I was pleased with myself, and I expected Pappy to be pleased with the job of teaching he had done. But when I turned, he was frowning.

"Take that silly grin off your face," he said roughly. "Sure you can shoot, but there's nothing so damned wonderful about that. I could teach the dumbest state policeman in Texas to shoot the same way, if I had the time. You just learn faster than others, that's all."

I didn't know what was wrong with him. He had worked from sunup to sundown for two days teaching me to shoot, and now that I had finally caught the knack of it, it made him mad.

Then his face softened a little and he looked at me soberly. "Now don't get your back up, son. I'm just trying to tell you that knowing how to shoot and draw isn't enough. Boothills are full of men who could outdraw and outshoot both of us. Shooting a man who's as good as you are, and shooting a pasteboard box, are two different things. Look. . . ."

He drew his pistols and held them out to me butts first.

"What do you want me to do?" I asked.

"Is this the way you'd disarm a man? Make him hand over his pistols butts first?"

"Sure," I said.

"Then take them."

I reached for them. The pistols whirled almost too fast to see, with no warning, no twist of the hand. With his fingers in the trigger guards, Pappy had flipped the pistols over, forward, cocking the hammers as they went around. In a split second — as long as it takes a man to die — he had whirled the .44's all the way around, cocked them, and snapped, with both muzzles against my chest.

The pistols were empty. Pappy had seen

to that beforehand. If they had been loaded I would have died without ever knowing how. My mouth had suddenly gone dry. I swallowed to get my stomach out of my throat.

Pappy holstered one pistol and casually began to load the other. "I said it once before," he said. "When it comes to guns, a man is never good enough. Now get your blanket roll together. We've stayed in one place too long already."

That night it rained, but we moved anyway, because Pappy said we had already used more luck than Indian Territory allowed. That night it caught up with us.

First, we almost rode into a detail of cavalry and, later, a hunting party of Cheyennes that had strayed off the reservation. We pulled up in a thicket of scrub oak and waited for the Indians to pass. I looked at Pappy and his face was just a blur in the rain and darkness, and I swore at myself for not bringing a slicker when I left John's City.

Pappy said, "I don't like it. With Indians off the reservation, there's bound to be cavalry all over this part of the Territory. Two stray riders wouldn't have much of a chance getting to Kansas."

I said, "The cattle trail can't be far from here. We can move in that direction, and if the cavalry sees us we can tell them we're drovers, looking for strays."

Pappy gave a sudden shrug. He didn't think much of the idea, but, with cavalry and Indians on the other side of us, there wasn't anything else to do. Pappy didn't mention Buck Creyton, and neither did I. After the Indians had passed on in the darkness, behind a slanting gray sheet of rain, we began moving to the west.

I think I smelled coffee even before I heard the nervous bawling of the cattle. Steaming, soothing coffee to warm a man's insides, and Pappy and I both needed it. We pulled up on a rise and looked down at the flatland below that some outfit was using for bedground. A herd of what seemed to be a thousand or more cattle was milling restlessly, and above the beat of the rain we could hear the night watch crooning profanely.

But the thing that caught our attention was the coffee. We could see a fire going under a slant of canvas that we took to be the chuck wagon, and that was where the smell was coming from.

Pappy looked at me. "You ever see that outfit before?"

"I don't know. I can't see enough of it to tell."

We were both thinking how good a hot cup of coffee would taste. We sat for a moment with rain in our face, rain plastering our clothing, rain running off our hats and slithering down our backs and filling our boots. Without a word, we started riding toward the fire.

As we circled the herd I heard one of the night herders croon, "Get on it there, you no-account sonofabitch," to the tune of "The Girl I Left Behind Me." There were three or four men standing under the canvas where the coffee smell was coming from. Pappy and I left our horses beside the chuck wagon and ducked in under the canvas sheet.

"Can you spare a couple of cups of that?" Pappy said to the cook, nodding at the big tin coffee pot.

The cook, a grizzled old man half asleep, grunted and got two tin cups and poured. The other men looked at us curiously, probably wondering where the hell we came from and where we left our slickers. I took a swallow of the scalding coffee, and another man ducked in under the canvas, cursing and shaking water from his oilskin rain hat. He looked at me and said:

"Well, I'll be damned."

For a minute, I stopped breathing. The man was Bat Steuber, the remuda man I had met back at Red River Station. We had run onto the same outfit that Buck Creyton was working for.

CHAPTER 8

Bat Steuber looked at us for a long minute, but I couldn't tell what he was thinking. Finally he turned to the other men and said, "The boss says, every man in the saddle that's supposed to be on night watch."

Cursing, the men left one at a time, got on their horses, and rode toward the herd again. Bat got his coffee and came over to the edge of the canvas where Pappy and I had moved.

"Is this Pappy Garret?" he said to me.

"That's right."

For a moment, he looked at Pappy with a mixture of awe and admiration. "I'm glad to know you, Pappy. I've heard about you." Then he laughed abruptly. "As who hasn't?"

Pappy nodded, looking at me. Steuber's voice went down almost to a whisper as he turned to me again. "Kid, it looks like I got you in a mess of trouble without meaning to. He's after you now instead of Pappy. Me and my goddamned big mouth."

"Who's after me?" I said.

"Buck Creyton." Steuber wiped his face nervously. "Hell, kid, I wasn't trying to get you into trouble. I was just trying to get Buck cooled down. He wasn't worth a damn on the herd as long as that temper of his was boiling. Anyway, after you left that day Buck was hell-bent on a shoot-out with Pappy here. And I said, 'Hell, Buck, what makes you think Pappy Garret killed your brother? It don't stand to reason. He wouldn't have no call to shoot Paul for nothing — and you know damn good and well that your brother wasn't going to pick a fight with a man like Pappy.' "

Steuber wiped his face again. "That was all I said," he went on. "I remember Buck didn't say a word for a long time, and I could see him thinking about it, way at the back of those eyes of his. And finally he said, 'That goddamned punk kid.' "

I felt my insides freeze as I remembered those kill-crazy eyes of Buck Creyton's. Pappy didn't say anything. He didn't move.

I said, "Where's Creyton now?"

"Out with the herd somewhere." Steuber made a helpless gesture. "Hell, kid, I'm sorry. . . ."

"Forget it," I said. "If you see him, tell

him the punk kid is down at the chuck wagon. Tell him if he wants to shoot off his mouth to do it to my face."

I could feel Pappy stiffen. Bat Steuber's eyes flew wide and he searched around for something to say, but the words wouldn't come. After a minute he made that same helpless gesture again. "All right, kid, if that's the way you want it." He ducked out into the rain.

Pappy said flatly, "Now that was a damn-fool thing to do."

I said, "Maybe. But a showdown has got to come sometime, and it might as well be now. I should have told him that first day when he was gunning for you, but I guess I lost my guts for a minute."

"You're not ready for a man like Crey-ton," Pappy said. "Now get that red horse of yours and we'll ride toward Kansas."

"And get taken by the cavalry?"

I looked at Pappy and his eyes were sober and sad. I said, "It's no good like this, Pappy. I appreciate what you've done for me, but you can't fight my fights for me. Remember what you said: 'A man does his own killing, and that's enough'? Well, this is between me and Buck Creyton. I don't want to go along for a month, or six months, or a year, looking over my shoulder every time I

187

hear a sound and expecting Buck Creyton to be there. And sooner or later he *would* be there, and maybe by that time I'd have lost my guts again."

For a long moment Pappy didn't move, didn't say anything. Then, at last, he got out a soggy sack of tobacco and his corn-shuck papers and began rolling a cigarette. After he had finished, he handed the makings to me.

"If that's the way it has to be," he said, "then I can't help you. It'll be between just you and Buck."

We stood there watching the rain, listening to the crooning of the night watch, and the nervous bawling of the cattle. After a while, I got a rag from the cook, wiped my guns dry, and put in fresh cartridges. After that there was nothing to do but wait.

Pappy didn't try to change my mind again. I guess he knew what it was like to be hunted, not only by the law, but by other killers like himself. And he knew it was better to get it over with now before the slow rot of time ate your guts away.

There was no way of knowing how long it would take the word to get to Creyton, but it would get to him. All I had to do was stand here, and before long he would be coming after me. I couldn't tell if I was scared or not. I wasn't very curious about it. There was an emptiness in my belly, and a dull ache . . . and maybe I was scared, after all. But not so much of Buck Creyton. My mind kept going back to better days and better lands, and, no matter how I fought it, I couldn't keep my thoughts away from Laurin.

That was what I was afraid of, not of getting killed, but of leaving Laurin.

In the darkness, we heard the hurried sucking sound of soggy boots coming toward the chuck wagon. I turned quickly. Beside me, Pappy jerked out of the weary slouch that he had fallen into.

"Watch it, son," he said quietly. "Don't frame yourself against the firelight."

The boots came on. A blurred figure began to take shape in the rain, walking quickly and making sloshing sounds in the gummy mud. But it wasn't Buck Creyton. It was a man I had never seen before, in dripping, rattling oilskins. He ducked under the shelter and stood glaring angrily at us.

"Get the hell out of here," he said abruptly. "I don't know who you are, but you're not goin' to start a shootin' scrape and stampede a thousand head of steers. Not if I can help it."

Pappy said softly, "Now wait a minute.

189

We're not starting anything. We just dropped in for a hot cup of coffee."

The man spat. "Like hell," he said. "You ride up and in ten minutes the whole camp's in an uproar." He looked at Pappy. "You ever hear of Buck Creyton?"

"I heard of him," Pappy said.

"He's comin' after you," the man said, grinning suddenly. He looked as if he expected Pappy to turn pale and start running at the mention of Buck Creyton. When Pappy didn't move, his eyes were suddenly angry again.

Pappy began rolling another cigarette. "It's not me he's after," he said. Then he nodded at me. "It's him."

The man stared. He was a short, round, hard little Irishman, with a baby-pink face and a blue-red nose. The herd's trail boss, I guessed. He didn't believe that an eighteen-year-old kid would stand still when he knew that a man like Creyton was gunning for him. He wheeled back on Pappy, about to call him a liar, when there was the sound of boots again, coming out of the darkness.

"The firelight, son," Pappy said softly. "Don't frame yourself."

I moved away, to the edge of the canvas shelter.

"Further," Pappy said.

190

I moved out into the rain. The rain hit my face like slender silver spikes driving out of a black nothingness. I felt empty and all alone out there, away from the fire's warmth, the canvas's shelter, Pappy's friendliness. There was just me and the night and the rain, and the sound of boots coming toward me. I thought: This is the way it had to be, Laurin. You understand that, don't you?

There was little comfort in the night's answer. The boots were getting closer. From the corner of my eye I could see Pappy standing there under the shelter, looking into the darkness. And the pink-faced little trail boss, with his mouth working angrily, but no sound coming out. The sound of the boots stopped. A voice came out of the night.

"Pappy, I want to see that killing little bastard you ride with."

I thought I could see Pappy smile. A sad, forlorn smile. "I reckon you'll see him, Buck, if you just keep walking."

"Where is he? Hid out to shoot me in the back, the way he did Paul?"

I heard myself saying, "I'm not hid out. I'm here in the rain, just like you are. And I didn't shoot your brother in the back. But I shot him."

I heard him swearing. "You won't shoot anybody else, punk. Not after tonight."

He started walking forward again, slowly now, carefully. I suppose I should have stayed where I was, stood still, with my pistols out. That way I could have followed the sound, and that would have cut down Creyton's advantages. But suddenly I didn't want any advantage. Pappy never asked for one. All he ever asked for was an even break, and I could get that here in the darkness. I started walking toward the sound.

I heard Pappy give a grunt of dismay. The trail boss said hoarsely, "My God, stop it! This is crazy!"

But we didn't stop. It couldn't be stopped now. With every step we got closer together and I expected to see him. My eyes began to jump from peering so hard, into the darkness. I didn't dare close them for an instant, even to blink away the water that was caught on my lashes. An instant was all it took with a man like Buck Creyton.

Pappy, and the trail boss, and the flickering firelight seemed to fade off into the distance and disappear completely. There was just me and a sound out there in the night. I wondered if Creyton had drawn yet. I wondered if that sighting-before-shooting technique of Pappy's worked in the rain.

Would anything work in the rain? This was a hell of a place for a gun fight, in the rain and darkness where you couldn't see anything. I thought: If you don't stop thinking about it, Buck Creyton's going to spill your guts in the mud. And then I saw him looming out of the darkness.

He looked as big as a mountain. He had his slicker pulled back behind the butts of his pistols and water was pouring in a sheer veil off the brim of his hat. His face shone faintly over the shapeless bulk of his body, as cold and distant as the moon. I imagined that I could see those icy eyes of his. But that was only imagination. Everything happened too fast, and it was too dark, to make out details.

His hands were just a blur going after his pistols, and I thought: He's fast. He's fast, all right. Pappy himself, on the best day he ever saw, was never any faster than that. Then everything in my mind became crystal clear and painfully sharp. It was that instant in a lifetime that a few people experience once, and most not at all — that instant of walking the razor-sharp edge of time and space, knowing that if you fall there is nothing but disaster all around you. Even my hearing was tuned sharper than the best-bred hunting dog's. I imagined that I could hear every raindrop hit. I could hear the double clicks as the hammers of Creyton's pistols were jerked back. And I thought: So this is the way it is. It's almost worth getting killed just to be a part of the excitement of dying. And then the night exploded into sound and fire.

I was vaguely aware of the pistols in my hands, and the roaring in my ears drowning all other sound. It was almost like being drunk, but no man had ever been drunk the way I was for that instant. Not on anything that came out of a bottle. For that moment I wasn't afraid of Buck Creyton, nor of any man on earth. I just held my guns and they did the rest, one crash crowding another until the night was crazy with sound. And after a time there were hollow, empty clicks as hammers fell on empty chambers, and I looked up ahead and there was only a shapeless hulk on the ground where Buck Creyton had been standing. I stood there gasping for breath, as if I had been running hard until my lungs couldn't take it any longer. And over the monotonous beat of the rain, I could hear the trail boss saying, "My God! My God!" over and over, as if he had to say something and those were the only two words he knew.

From far away, it seemed, I heard the

sound of alarm and the crazy bawling and the pound of hoofs. And a voice in the darkness shouted, "Stampede!" and the running boots headed for the chuck wagon suddenly stopped, wheeled, and ran toward the remuda pen for the horses. Over it all, the trail boss was bellowing wildly, but it all seemed far away and no concern of mine.

Pappy came out from under the shelter, looking at me strangely. Then he went over to what was left of Buck Creyton.

"Jesus Christ, son," Pappy said, "did you have to shoot him all to pieces?"

"I couldn't stop," I said. "I started shooting and something got ahold of me, and I couldn't stop."

Pappy looked at me again in that strange way. I couldn't tell what was behind those gray expressionless eyes of his. I couldn't tell if he was glad or sorry that it had worked out the way it had. For a moment, as he looked at me, I thought there was fear in those eyes. But I must have been mistaken about that.

"Do you feel like riding?" Pappy said at last.

"Sure," I said. "But why should we ride anywhere?"

He jerked his head toward the bedground where all the noise and commotion was going on. All hell was breaking loose, but I was just beginning to become conscious of it. It was almost like returning suddenly from a long visit in a strange place, and it took a while to get used to things as you used to know them. The cattle had broken toward the north, running blind and wild with fear. The riders, some of them just in the underwear they had been sleeping in, were riding hard on the flanks, trying to turn them.

"After starting this ruckus," Pappy said, "the least we can do is help them turn the herd."

Pappy started in an awkward half-lope toward his horse beside the chuck wagon. In a moment I came out of it. I ran toward Red, and on the way I passed the bloody, shapeless form that had been Buck Creyton a few minutes before. He lay twisted, in the mud, looking straight up, with the rain in his face. There were bright, shimmering puddles forming all around him.

I hit the saddle hard, and Red switched his head in angry protest. He didn't want to move. He had lulled himself into a kind of stupor there in the rain, and he just wanted to be let alone. I drove the iron to him and he reared sharply. Finally I pulled him around and he fell into a quick, ground-eating run to the north.

We caught Pappy on the herd's flank just as the break began to settle down to a real stampede. There wasn't time to be scared, the way they say you always are after a fight. There was just the blind race along the flanks of the herd, and once in a while I could feel Red slide and fight for his footing again in the mud, and I tried not to think what would happen if he put a hoof down on a loose rock or into a prairie-dog hole. Red and Pappy's big black spurted ahead of most of the other riders. Up ahead, I could hear the trail boss yelling and cursing.

He was trying to turn them by himself as Pappy and I came up alongside him. He drove his rugged little paint into the van of the stampede. Leaning far over his pony he shoved the muzzle of his pistol behind the shoulders of the lead steer and fired.

The big animal thundered down, rolling and churning the mud, slowing the herd's rush. Without looking back to see who we were, he roared, "Turn 'em, goddammit!"

I thought I could make out that faint grin of Pappy's as he drove his big black into the point of the herd. I shoved Red in after him, and the trail boss came in on our heels. The startled cattle began to slow down their crazy rush for nowhere. The point began to give, began to edge to the left as Pappy and the trail boss pushed in, yelling and firing their pistols over the animals' heads.

There wasn't much to it after the point began to give. We cut them over and headed them back until we had two columns of cattle going in opposite directions; then the riders came up and milled them in a wide circle.

After the riders got the mill going, there was nothing for me and Pappy to do. We pulled up the slope a way to let our horses blow after the hard run. I noticed then, for the first time, that it had stopped raining.

"One steer lost," I said. "It could have been worse."

Pappy looked at me. "One steer and one rider," he said dryly. He nodded toward the bottom of the slope to where a rider was coming toward us. It was the trail boss.

Surprisingly, he didn't seem mad this time. He just looked relieved to get his herd under control with the loss of only one steer. He pulled up in front of us, mopping his face with a rain-soaked bandanna.

"By God," he said wearily, "I ought to turn the two of you over to the bluebellies."

Pappy straightened in the saddle. "What makes you think the bluebellies want us?"

The little Irishman laughed roughly.

"You're Pappy Garret, the boys tell me. And this kid's name's Cameron, ain't it?" Without waiting for an answer, he took a folded, soggy square of paper from his hip pocket. It was too dark to read, but a sinking feeling in my stomach told me what it was.

"Reward," the trail boss said pleasantly. "For killin' off some bluebelly cavalry down in northern Texas. Ten thousand for Garret, five for the kid. Here, read it for yourself."

Pappy made no move to take the paper. "Are you aiming to make a try for that reward money?" he asked softly.

The trail boss laughed abruptly. "Hell, no." Then his voice got serious. "It's no concern of mine if the army wants to take you in. I'm short of hands and good horses. From the way you two jumped in and turned that herd, it looks like my problem is taken care of. That is, if you want a job."

Pappy looked at me. He was thinking the same thing I was. "I kind of figured," he said, "that you'd be sore because the boy killed off one of your riders."

The trail boss snorted. "It was small loss. Creyton was trouble from the first day I signed him on. He thought he was Godamighty with them two pistols of his . . . and I guess he had everybody else thinking it until tonight." He looked at me with much the same expression that I had seen in Pappy's eyes. "I'll tell you the truth," he said. "I never expected you to beat Buck Creyton, son. I was expecting we'd be burying a kid of a boy in the morning." He shrugged. "But I guess you never know."

He pulled his paint around and studied the herd for a minute. "Think it over," he said. "If you want to sign up, I'll see you at the chuck wagon for breakfast."

He rode down the slope again and into the darkness. I looked at Pappy and he was shaking his head slowly from side to side. "I guess it's like the man says," he said soberly. "You never know."

It was too good a thing to pass up. With fifteen thousand dollars on our heads, every soldier in the Territory was a potential bounty hunter. The next morning we were at the chuck wagon and Bass Hagan, the hard pink-faced little trail boss, signed us on. Somebody must have buried Buck Creyton, but there was no mention of it at breakfast. There was no talk of any kind, for that matter. The riders regarded Pappy with a kind of dumb awe, and me . . . I couldn't be sure just what they were thinking about me. I could feel their eyes on me when they didn't think I was looking. Curious eyes, mixed with a kind of fear, I thought. They ate their breakfast quickly and silently as a cold sun began to come up in the east. Then, with elaborate casualness, they sauntered down to the remuda pen to get their horses.

It took a while to get used to that kind of treatment, but I finally did, as one long, weary, dust-filled day dragged into another. The men let me and Pappy strictly alone. And I began to appreciate how Pappy had lived all these years with that reputation of his. It was like being by yourself on the moon. You couldn't have been more alone. In every man you looked at, you saw that same mixture of curiosity and fear — like men partially hypnotized by a caged and especially deadly breed of snake. They couldn't take their eyes off it. But they knew better than to get into the cage with it.

That was the way it was after getting a reputation by killing a man like Buck Creyton.

Bass Hagan, the trail boss, was the only man who didn't seem to be afraid of us, but he spent most of his time up in the van, and Pappy and I ate dust back in the drag. And it wasn't long before I learned to hate the nights, when time came for sleeping. I learned to sleep the way Pappy did, always keeping a corner of my mind open, never letting myself slip into complete unconsciousness. I learned to sleep — if you could call it sleeping — on my back, with a cocked pistol in my hand. I kept thinking of that reward money. I wondered how long it would be before somebody tried to collect.

I learned a lot of things in those days as we pushed from the Canadian up to North Cottonwood in Kansas. Pappy was my teacher. A little at a time, every day, he showed me the little tricks that men like us had to know to stay alive. The first rule, the most important rule of all, was to trust no one. Accept it as truth that every man you met was scheming to kill you, that every footstep behind you was a man ready to shoot you in the back. Never get caught off guard. Never relax. Never take more than two or three drinks, and let women alone. Never let anyone do you a favor without paying for it, never become obligated to anybody.

And that was only the beginning. He coached me on how to enter a door, any door. First you listened; if it sounded all right, then you stepped inside fast, with a quick step to the side so as to get your back against a wall and not frame yourself against the light. There was a certain toe-heel way to walk when you didn't want to be heard, and a way to block your spur rowels to keep them from jangling. Little things, all of them. Things that ordinary men would pay no attention to, but with Pappy they were matters of life and death.

I learned to value my pistols above all other possessions, and to take care of them before seeing to anything else. My horse came next, almost as important as the pistols. I learned that my own comfort was almost of no importance at all. A thousand things came ahead of that, if I wanted to keep living.

What Pappy had to teach me, I learned fast, the way I learned to shoot. Already, among the trail hands, there was talk of Davis being removed from the governor's chair in Austin, and that meant that military rule and the Davis police would go with him. It was important that I learn everything that Pappy could teach me, because I had to stay alive, to go back to Texas.

North Cottonwood was the settling-up place for the cattlemen before going the last thirty-five miles to Abilene. It was there that the riders were paid off and discharged, unless they happened to belong to the drover's own outfit, and then they went on to the railhead with the herd. It was there that all the scrawny and sickly cattle were cut out of the herd and left to fatten before going to market. It was a crazy patchwork of wagons, and dust, and bawling cattle, and cow camps. Punchers who hadn't had a drop to drink and hadn't seen a woman for more than two months began peeling off their filthy trail clothing, bathing, shaving, and putting on their one clean pair of serge pants that they had brought in their saddle-bags all the way from the Rio Grande, maybe.

I could see Pappy's eyes take on new life after we finally got the herd rounded up on a bedground that suited Bass Hagan.

"This is the place, son," he said. "You haven't seen a town until you've seen Abilene."

He even found a clean pair of pants and a shirt with all the buttons on it, and put them on to celebrate the occasion. But Pappy got a jolt that afternoon as the riders were being paid off. Bass Hagan called us over to one of the supply wagons where they had set up headquarters.

"Now, what the hell?" Pappy said.

I said, "Maybe we're so good he wants to hire us for another trail drive."

Pappy grunted. Trail driving was work, and he had had enough of that to last him for a while. What money Pappy needed he could usually get over a poker table.

But we went over anyway. Hagan was slicked and duded up in a fancy outfit that he had been saving for the end of the trail. He was just cinching up a big bay, the best horse in the remuda, when Pappy and I got there.

"I want you boys to stay with the herd," Hagan said without looking around. "It'll mean extra pay for a couple of days. I've got to ride into town on business."

Pappy said, "We don't need the extra pay. We just signed up as far as North Cottonwood."

The trail boss turned slowly, frowning. "I figured I done you boys a favor by hiring you on and getting you through Indian Territory. But if you figure it's too damn much to ask, staying over a couple of days . . ."

Pappy glanced at me. Sure, Hagan had done us a favor, but we had earned our money on that trail drive. I could see Pappy's face grow longer. "Never let anyone do you a favor without paying for it," he had said. "Never become obligated to anyone."

Pappy shrugged. "All right, Bass. I guess we can stay here a couple of days. What do you want us to do?"

Hagan brightened. "Nothing special, just

205

help my other riders take care of the herd till I get back." He swung up on the bay, grinning quietly. As we watched him put his spurs to the bay and lope off to the north, an idea got stuck in my mind and I couldn't get it out.

I said, "Something just occurred to me. Do you think Hagan would think enough of fifteen thousand dollars to try to get us arrested?"

Pappy took a long time rolling one of his corn-shuck cigarettes. He held a match to it thoughtfully, handing the makings to me. At last he smiled that sad half-smile that I had come to expect. "I think I've said it before, son," he said. "You learn fast."

But we stayed on with the herd, and, if Pappy was worried, it didn't show on that long face of his. We didn't mention Hagan again that day, but when night came we fell automatically into a routine, that we had worked out, of one sleeping and one watching.

Once Pappy said, "Money is a funny thing. The root of all evil, they say. Men steal for it, kill for it, lie for it . . ." He inhaled deeply on a cigarette. "Money," he said again. "I never had much of it myself. I could have hooked up with the Bassett gang once when they was robbing the Confederate payrolls. If I'd done it, maybe I'd have been a rich man now."

He laughed abruptly, without humor. "My ma always taught me that it was a sin to steal. I never stole a dime in my life . . ."

Pappy's voice trailed off. He didn't know how to say it, but I thought I knew what was going on in his mind. I had thought about it too, since I saw that reward poster with my name on it. Most men got something out of their crimes — maybe not much, when they stood on the gallows thinking about it, waiting for the floor to drop out from under them, but something. Men like me and Pappy, we didn't get anything. All the money we had was the thirty-odd dollars that Hagan had paid us for the trail job. All the satisfaction we had was that of knowing that we were faster with guns that most men, and that wasn't much of a satisfaction when you thought of what other men had. Security, homes, wives. Things that Pappy could never have. And — I had to face it now — things that I would never have if I didn't somehow fight my way out of the crazy whirl of killing that seemed to have no beginning and no end.

The thought of that scared me. It made me sick all the way down to the bottom of my stomach when I thought of ending up the way Pappy was bound to end. Without Laurin. Without anything. Until now, I had been telling myself that there really wasn't anything to worry about, all I had to do was hold out until I could get a free trial in Texas. But now I wasn't sure. Paul Creyton, the policemen, the cavalryman, Buck Creyton — after each one I had told myself that there wouldn't be any more killing. I could still say it, but I couldn't believe the words any more.

"I never stole a dime in my life," Pappy said again, as if just thinking about that particular clean part of his life made him feel better.

I found myself hoping desperately that Bass Hagan would let well enough alone and just tend to his cattle business in Abilene. I thought bitterly: If they would just let us alone . . . If Paul Creyton hadn't tried to steal my horse, if the bluebelly hadn't killed Pa . . .

But it was too late for tears. We couldn't change the past — nor the future either, for that matter. If Hagan had it in his head to try for the reward money, nothing would stop him. If it wasn't now, it would be later.

CHAPTER 9

The next morning was hot and hazy with dust from ten thousand stamping cattle scattering as far as you could see in any direction. There wasn't anything for Pappy and me to do. Hagan's regular riders were taking care of the herd and remuda, and guarding the wagons. I thought: It seems crazy as hell for Hagan to pay good money for riders he doesn't need. Unless, of course, he was figuring to get his money back, and some more with it. I watched Pappy plundering around in one of the supply wagons, and after a while he climbed down with a towel over his shoulder and a bar of soap in his hand.

"I figure we might as well wash up," he said with a thin grin, "as long as there doesn't seem to be any work for us to do."

I said, "Don't you think one of us better keep watch?" We still hadn't mentioned Hagan, but he was never far out of our minds.

Pappy shrugged. "We can watch from the creek. Maybe we've just got a case of the jumps. Anyway, we need a bath. We can't ride into Abilene looking like a pair of saddle tramps."

Pappy was the careful one; if he thought it was all right, then it was all right. We went down to the remuda herd and cut out Red and Pappy's big black and got them saddled. The creek was only about a hundred yards back of our wagons, but a horseman never walks anywhere if he can ride.

We left the horses down by the water, and I took my place under a rattling cottonwood while Pappy bathed first. Nothing happened that I could see. I had a clear view of the herd and wagons, and everything was going on as usual. Behind me, I could hear Pappy splashing around and grunting at the shock of cold water. After a while he climbed up the bank where I was, wearing his new serge pants and clean shirt. But he didn't look much different, with that scraggly crop of whiskers still on his face.

"No sign of Hagan yet?" he asked.

I shook my head.

"Go on and take your bath," he said, handing me the wet bar of yellow lye soap. "I'll let you know if we've got company."

I peeled off my clothes and waded out

knee deep in the bitter cold water. I didn't have a change of clothes. That was something else I forgot to bring from John's City, along with a slicker. Well, I had over thirty dollars in my pocket. That would buy me some clothes in Abilene — providing nobody got too set on keeping us out of Abilene.

In the meantime, I washed the clothes I had, lathering them with the lye soap, then weighting them down to the bottom of the stream with a rock while I washed myself. I was grimy from top to bottom, not just my hands and feet and face, like it used to be on Saturday nights when Ma put the big wooden washtub in the kitchen and filled it for me and Pa. I scrubbed hard, using sand on my elbows and knees when the soap wouldn't do the job. I didn't feel naked until I got all the dirt off. After I had finished, I felt like I must have polluted the stream for ten miles down.

After I had sloshed my clothes around to get the soap out, wrung them out and hung them on a bush to dry, I went downstream to take care of Red. He wasn't as dirty as I had been, but I rinsed off some caked mud on his legs and rubbed him down and he looked better.

"You about finished down there, son?"

Pappy called.

"Sure," I said. "I was just sprucing Red up a little."

"You better get your clothes on," Pappy said with a mildness that still deceived me sometimes. "It looks like we're going to have company, after all."

I stiffened in the cold water. Then I splashed over to the edge and went over to the bush where my clothes were. They weren't dry, but they weren't as wet as they had been the night of the rain — the night I had killed Buck Creyton. I put them on the way they were, stuffed my feet in my boots, and buckled on the .44's.

As I went clawing my way up the bank, Pappy said, "Keep down, son. We don't want to tell them anything they don't already know."

I raised my head carefully over the edge of the bank, the way Pappy was doing. Sure enough, it was Hagan and four other men that I'd never seen before. All of them were heeled up with guns. Hagan was the only one not carrying a rifle in his saddle boot.

"Who are they?" I said.

"Jim Langly's men."

I shot Pappy a glance. Langly was the marshal of Abilene.

I said, "I thought the marshal was a friend

212

of yours."

Pappy smiled that smile of his, but this time it seemed sadder than usual. "That was a mistake I made," he said quietly. "You never know who your friends are until you get a price on your head."

"What are you going to do?"

"I don't know," Pappy said slowly. "I haven't decided yet."

We lay there for a long moment watching Hagan call one of the herders over. The man pointed toward the creek, evidently in answer to a question. The man went away, and Hagan called the four Langly men together and talked for a minute. Then the men fanned out, taking up positions inside the covered supply wagons.

"Well, that's about as clear as a man could want it," Pappy said.

I felt myself tightening up. The rattle of the cottonwood seemed louder than it had a few minutes before. Smells were sharper. Even my eyes were keener.

"That bastard," I said. "That lousy bastard."

"Hagan?"

"Who else?"

Pappy seemed to think it over carefully. "I guess we really can't blame Hagan much," he said. "Fifteen thousand is a lot of money for a few minutes' work — especially if you don't have any idea how dangerous work like that can be." He paused for a minute. "But Jim Langly . . . We've been good friends for years. This is a hell of a thing for Jim to do."

He still didn't sound mad, but more hurt than anything.

"What are you going to do?" I asked again.

After a long wait, Pappy said, "I think maybe we'll ride up the creek a way, and then make for Abilene and talk to Jim."

"You're not going to let Hagan get away with this, are you?" I was suddenly hot inside. I had forgotten that last night I had promised myself no more trouble.

"We can't buck four saddle guns," Pappy said.

I knew he was right, but my hands ached to get at Hagan's throat. I wanted to see that pink face of his turn red, and then blue, and then purple. But I choked the feeling down and the effort left me empty. It always has to be somebody, I thought. Now it's Hagan, and Langly. Why can't they just let us alone?

Slowly, Pappy began sliding down the bank. His eyes looked tired and very old.

We went upstream as quietly as we could, scattering drinking cattle and horses, and once in a while coming upon a naked man lathering himself with soap. We rode for maybe a mile in the creek bed, until we were pretty sure that nobody in the Hagan camp could see us; then we pulled out in open country and headed north.

Pappy rode stiffly in the saddle, not looking one way or the other. After a while the hurt look went out of his eyes, and a kind of smoky anger banked up like sullen thunderheads.

We left North Cottonwood behind; and I wondered vaguely how long it would be before Hagan and his lawdogs would get tired of waiting in those covered wagons and send somebody down to the creek to see what had happened to us. Maybe they already had.

I tried to keep my mind blank. I tried to push Hagan and Langly out of my brain, but they hung on and ate away at me like a rotting disease. As we rode, the morning got to be afternoon and a dazzling Kansas sun moved over to the west and beat at us like a blowtorch. Gradually the monotony of silent march lulled me into a stupor, and I found myself counting every thud as Red put a hoof down, and cussing Bass Hagan with every breath.

Actually, it wasn't Hagan in particular that

I was cursing, but mankind in general. The thousands of greedy, money-loving bastards like Hagan who were never satisfied to take care of their own business and let it go at that. They were like a flock of vultures feeding on other people's misery. They were like miserable coyotes sniffing around a sick cow, waiting until the animal was too weak to fight back and then pouncing and killing. I had enough hate for all the Hagans. The thousands of them. All the bastards who wouldn't let us alone, who insisted on getting themselves killed. And every time they insisted, it put a bigger price on our heads.

I remember looking over at Pappy once and wondering if he had ever thought of it that way. Pappy, who had never stolen a dime in his life, who had never wanted to hurt anybody except when it was a matter of life or death for himself — I wondered if he felt trapped the way I did, if he could feel the net drawing a little tighter every time some damned fool forced him to kill. If Pappy ever felt that way, he had never talked about it. He wasn't much of a man with words. And then it occurred to me that maybe that was the reason he was the kind of man he was. Being unable to depend on words, maybe he had been forced to let his guns do the talking.

Then, out of nowhere, Laurin came into my brain and cooled the heat of anger and helpless frustration, the way it happened so many times. When everything seemed lost, then Laurin would enter into my thoughts and everything was all right again. I'll be coming back, I promised. And I could almost see that hopeful, wide-eyed smile of hers. They can't keep me away from you, I said silently. You're the only important thing in my life. The only real thing. Everything's going to be all right. You'll see.

I looked up suddenly and Pappy was giving me that curious look. I felt my face warm. I had been speaking my thoughts out loud.

"Well?" I said.

"Nothing, son," Pappy said soberly. "Not a thing."

It was late in the afternoon when we finally sighted Abilene. The noise, the bawling of cattle, the shrill screams of locomotive whistles around the cattle pens, the fitful cloud of dust that surged over the place like a restless shroud gave you an idea of what the town was like long before you got close enough to be part of it. Over to the west we could see new herds coming up from North Cottonwood, heading for the dozen of giant cattle pens on the edge of town. Pappy and I circled the cattle pens, and the combined noise of prodded steers and locomotives and hoarsely shouting punchers was like something out of another world. It was worse than a trail drive. It was like nothing I had ever seen before. I had never seen a train before, and I kept looking back long after we had passed the pens, watching the giant black engine with white steam spurting in all directions, and the punchers jabbing the frightened cattle with poles, forcing them through the loading gates and into the slatted cattle cars.

Then we came into the town itself, which was mostly one long street — Texas Street, they called it — of saloons and barbershops and gambling parlors and dance halls. Some of the places were all four wrapped in one, with extra facilities upstairs for the fancy women who leaned out of the windows shouting at us as we rode by. The street was a mill of humanity and animals and wagons and hacks of every kind I ever saw, and a lot I had never seen before. Every man seemed to be cursing, and every jackass braying, every wagon squeaking, and every horse stomping. The whole place was a restless, surging pool of sound and excitement that got hold of you like a fever.

So this was Pappy's town. I didn't know if

I liked it or not, but I didn't think I did. I didn't think the town would ever quiet down long enough to let a person draw an easy breath and be a part of it.

I couldn't help wondering what Pappy was going to do, now that he was here. Would he be crazy enough to walk up and kill the marshal of a town like this? I couldn't believe that Pappy would try a thing like that, not unless he knew he had some backing from somewhere. More backing than I would be able to give him.

But his face didn't tell me anything. A few curious eyes watched us as we pushed our way up the street, but most of the men were too intent on their own personal brand of hell-raising to pay any attention to us. At last Pappy pulled his big black in at the hitching rack near the middle of the block. I pulled Red in, pushing to make room between a bay and a roan.

We hitched and stepped up to the plank walk, but before we went into the bar that Pappy was headed for, I said, "Pappy, don't you think this is damn foolishness, trying to take the marshal of a place like this?"

He looked at me flatly. "You don't have to go with me, son. This is just between Jim and me."

"I'm not trying to get out of anything," I

said. "It just looks crazy to me, that's all."

Some men had stopped on the plank walk to look at us. Perhaps they recognized Pappy, for they didn't loiter after Pappy had raked them with that flat gaze of his.

"You go buy yourself some clothes," Pappy said quietly. "I can take care of this."

He seemed to forget that I was there. He turned and pushed through the batwings of a place called the Mule's Head Bar, going in quick in that special way of his, and then stepping over with his back to the wall. I didn't think about it, I just went in after him. Somehow, Pappy's fights had got to be my fights. I hadn't forgotten the way he had taken care of the cavalry for me that time at Daggert's cabin.

We stood there on either side of the door, Pappy sweeping the place in one quick glance, taking in everything, missing nothing. "Well, son," he said, "as long as you've dealt yourself in, you might as well watch my back for me."

I said, "Sure, Pappy." But it looked like it was going to be a job. The saloon was a big place with long double bars, one on each side of the building. There were trail hands two and three deep along the bars seeing how fast they could spend their hard-earned cash, and the tables in the middle of the floor were crowded with more trail hands, and saloon girls, and slickers, and pimps, and just plain hardcases with guns on both hips and maybe derringers in their vest pockets.

Down at the end of the bars there was a fish-eyed young man with rubber fingers playing a tinny-sounding piano. The tune was "Dixie," and a dozen or so cowhands were ganged around singing: "Oh, have you heard the latest news, Of Lincoln and his Kangaroos . . ." One of the million versions of the tune born in the South during the war.

The gambling tables — faro, stud, draw, chuck-a-luck, seven-up, every device ever dreamed up to get money without working for it — were back in the rear of the place. That was what Pappy made for. I hung close to the doors as Pappy wormed his way between the tables and chairs, trying to keep my eyes on the gallery — I didn't intend to let a gallery fool me again — and on the men with the most guns. Before Pappy had taken a dozen steps, you could feel a change in the place. It wasn't much at first. Maybe a man would be talking or laughing, then he'd look up and see those awful, deadly eyes of Pappy's, and the talking or laughing would suddenly be left hanging on the rafters. One after another was affected that way, suddenly stricken with silence as Pappy moved by. By the time he had reached the gambling part of the saloon, the place was almost quiet.

I moved over to the bar on my left, keeping one eye on Pappy and the other on the big bar mirror to see what was going on behind me. Most of the men had turned away from the bar now, watching Pappy with puzzled expressions on their faces, as if they couldn't understand how a scrawny, haggard-looking man like that could draw so much attention. Then mouths began to move and you could almost feel the electricity in the place as the word passed along.

Somebody spoke to the man beside me. Automatically, the man turned to me and hissed, "It's Pappy Garret! He's after somebody, sure's hell!"

The men around the piano sang: "Our silken banners wave on high; For Southern homes, we'll fight and die." Still to the tune of "Dixie." Their voices died out on the last word. The piano went on for a few bars, but pretty soon it died out, too. All eyes seemed to be on Pappy.

I didn't have any trouble picking Jim Langly out of the crowd. His eyes were wider, and his face was whiter, and he was

222

having a harder time of breathing than anybody else in the place. When he had looked up from his poker hand and had seen Pappy coming toward him, he'd looked as if he was seeing a ghost. And maybe he was, as far as he was concerned. Maybe he'd figured that Pappy would be dead on a creek bank by now, and all he had to do was wait for the reward money to come in and think up ways to beat Hagan out of his share.

He started to get up, then thought better of it, and sat down again. You could almost see him take hold of himself, force himself to be calm. He laid his cards face down on the table, fanning them carefully.

"Why, hello, Pappy," he said pleasantly.

He was a big, slack-faced man wearing the gambler's uniform of black broadcloth and white ruffled shirt. He wasn't wearing side guns, but there was a bulge under his left arm that looked about right for a .38 and a shoulder holster.

"Hello, Jim," Pappy said quietly. "I guess you didn't expect to see me coming in like this, did you?"

I thought I saw the marshal's face get a little whiter. "Nobody ever knows when to expect Pappy Garret," he smiled. One of his poker partners wiped his face uncomfortably, gathered in his chips, and eased away from the table. Langly pushed the empty chair out with his boot. "Sit down, Pappy. It's been a long time."

Pappy shook his head soberly. Carefully, I moved down the bar, looking for a place where I could do the impossible of covering the saloon with two guns. I saw that Langly was having trouble again getting his words out.

"What can I do for you, Pappy? Is there any trouble?"

"Maybe, Jim," Pappy murmured.

Marshal Langly wiped his face with a neat, clean handkerchief. "What is it, Pappy? What do you want?"

"I came to kill you," Pappy said softly.

The words were soft, but they hit Langly like a sledge. You could hear the wind go out of him, see his guts leak out. He groped for words, but there weren't any there.

"That's the way it goes with men like us, Jim. You tried to kill me and failed. A man only gets one chance in this business."

"Pappy, what the hell's wrong with you? I don't know what you're talking about!"

"Sure you do, Jim," Pappy went on in that velvety voice of his. "Hagan, our trail boss, came to you yesterday with a proposition. A profitable proposition for you, Jim — maybe

224

fifteen thousand dollars, if you could figure out a way to keep Hagan from getting his split of the reward."

"How could I do anything to you, Pappy? Hell, I've been here all day playing draw."

"But not your deputies," Pappy said. "They're right on the job. The job you put them on."

The saloon seemed to be holding its breath. I glanced at faces around me. There were quizzical half-smiles on most of them, as if they thought it was all some kind of a big joke. I turned back to Pappy. I couldn't take my eyes off of him.

For a long moment he was silent, motionless. Langly was frozen. Then Pappy said, "You might as well draw, Jim."

The marshal's mouth worked. "Pappy, for God's sake!"

"I'll give you time to clear leather," Pappy went on, "before I make a move. That ought to make it about even."

"Pappy, listen to me!" The marshal was begging now, begging for his life. "Pappy, for God's sake, I had nothing to do with it!"

"I'll count to three," Pappy went on, as if he hadn't heard. Then something hard jabbed me in the small of the back.

I jumped, grunted instinctively. Pappy

stiffened, but he didn't turn around. "What's the matter, son?" he asked quietly.

I had to tell him.

"Somebody's got a gun in my back," I said. "I'm sorry, Pappy. I guess I'll never learn."

CHAPTER 10

I couldn't see who was holding the gun, and I didn't turn around to look. The slightest movement, I knew, would only get me a sudden trip to Boothill.

Marshal Langly started to breathe again. He stopped sweating and shaking, and his face began to get some color. Suddenly he sat back and laughed out of pure relief.

"Pappy Garret," he chuckled after he caught his breath. "The notorious gunman!" Then his voice barked. "Unbuckle your cartridge belts and drop your pistols to the floor!"

Or I would get a bullet in the back, his eyes said.

For an instant I wondered if Pappy really cared what happened to me, as long as he could take his revenge out on Langly. But I didn't have to wonder long. Wearily, he unbuckled the belts and the pistols dropped at his feet.

"All right, Jim," he said tiredly. "I guess you've got it going your way now."

Langly had his own .38 out now. "You bet I have, Pappy. I've got it going my way and that's the way it's going to stay." He sat back, looking pleased with himself. "You didn't think your old friend Jim Langly would be the one to bring you to your knees, did you? Well, you were wrong, Pappy. You haven't got any friends — not even that kill-crazy kid you've been riding with. Sooner or later he would have turned on you, because he's just the same as you are."

He was enjoying himself now. Him with a pistol in his hand and Pappy's .44's on the floor. And me with a gun in my back. He wasn't afraid of anything now. He was a hero and enjoying every minute of it. But the crowd in the saloon was still too stunned to be sure that is wasn't a joke.

"You know what you are, Pappy?" the marshal smiled. "You're a mad dog. You kill by instinct, the way a mad dog does. I'll be doing the whole country a favor by locking you up and turning you over to the Texas authorities."

My stomach sank. I might as well die here as on a carpetbag gallows.

But Pappy didn't move. He said, "I don't

suppose the price on my head had anything to do with it."

Langly went on smiling. He could afford to smile now. He got up from the table and said, "All right, Bass, take the kid's guns and we'll lock them up."

The man behind moved around in front. When he got around to face me I was too startled to guess what was going on in Pappy's mind. The man was Bass Hagan.

He must have come into Abilene right behind me and Pappy, but he hadn't used the same trail we had. He stood there with the pistol in my belly, grinning that wide grin of his.

"The pistols," he said. "Hand them over, kid."

And then I began to get it. Pappy still had his back turned to me, but I knew what he must be thinking. I reached very carefully for my right-hand pistol, slid it out of the holster.

"Butts first," Hagan grinned. He was the careful kind. He was standing back far enough so that I couldn't rush him, even if I was crazy enough to rush a man with a cocked pistol in his hand. "Just hand them over, kid," he said.

If he had known more about guns and gunmen he would have done as Langly had done, ordered me to unbuckle my belts. But he didn't know. I took the pistol by the barrel, slipping my finger into the trigger guard, and held it out. It had been a beautiful maneuver when Pappy had done it. But this time it wasn't Pappy. And the gun in my belly was loaded and cocked.

Maybe I would have handed the gun over if he hadn't been grinning. But he kept on grinning and I thought, There never would have been this trouble if it hadn't been for you. And my hand did the rest.

The pistol was just a blur as it whirled forward. The hammer snapped back as it hit my thumb on top of the turn, and fell forward.

I think Bass Hagan began to die before the bullet ever reached him. I could see death in his eyes even before the muzzle blast jarred the room, before the bullet slammed into his chest and he reeled back without ever pulling the trigger.

The shot affected the saloon customers like a stunning blow of a pole ax on a steer. They stood dumb, watching Hagan go to his knees and die, then fall on his face. Even Langly couldn't seem to move.

But Pappy could. He sliced across with the edge of his hand and sent the marshal's little .38 clattering to the floor. A split second was all it took. I wheeled instinctively to turn my pistol on Langly, but Pappy said sharply:

"No, son!"

For some reason, I held my fire. Nobody but Pappy could have stopped me then. But Pappy's voice did it. I held the hammer back and my finger relaxed a little on the trigger.

Pappy said, "He's not worth wasting a bullet on." But his eyes, not his voice, put the real bitterness into the words. "Come along, son," he said, picking up his guns. "I guess Abilene's not our town after all."

Well, if that was the way Pappy wanted it . . . I started toward the doors, moving sideways, trying to keep my eyes on both sides of me and on the bar mirror on the opposite wall. Then Pappy said:

"Just a minute, son. The marshal will be going with us."

I began to get it then. With the marshal dead, our chances of getting out of Abilene would be cut down to nothing. But with the marshal going with us, under the threat of sudden death if anybody tried to stop us, then maybe we could do it.

I waited, covering Pappy's retreat. Langly's mouth was working again. He looked as if he was going to be sick on the floor.

"Pappy, for God's sake, can't you take a

joke?" he said quickly. "You don't really think I'd turn you over to the Texas police, do you?"

Pappy's face didn't show a thing. He reached out with a clawlike hand, grabbed the front of the marshal's ruffled shirt, and gave him a shove toward the door. Then he paused for just a moment to address our stunned audience.

"I don't guess it will take a lot of figuring," he said, "to guess what will happen to the marshal if anybody tries to follow us out of town." He waited another moment to make sure that they had it clear. Then he said, "All right, son, let's be moving."

I waited at the doors, keeping the crowd covered, while Pappy got our horses in the street. He said something under his breath and Langly got on a gray mare that had been hitched beside Red. It was funny, in a way. Men with guns on both hips, pushing and shoving in both directions on the plank walk, and none of them bothering to give us a second look. I slammed the batwings then, turned and vaulted up to Red's back.

We fogged it down Texas Street in a wedge formation, Langley in the point and me and Pappy on both sides. Pappy let out an ear-splitting yell like a crazy man, then drew one pistol and emptied it in the air. But

Pappy wasn't so crazy. The crowd in the street, thinking we were drunk trail hands, scattered for the plank walks, and we had a clear road to travel out of Abilene.

"Make for the dust!" Pappy yelled, pointing toward the low-hanging red clouds rising up from a herd coming in for shipment. I crowded Langly on my side, turning him to the west. I looked back once as we went into the dust, but nobody was coming after us yet.

I didn't like the idea of making a getaway along the trail of incoming herds. Too many people could see us. But pretty soon night came on and we didn't have to depend on the dust for concealment. Then we swung to the west, Langly still in the middle.

At last we came to a creek, and we stopped there to let our horses blow. Pappy seemed to be in good spirits again. He kept looking at the marshal with that half-grin of his.

"Jim," he said, "it looks like your friends in Abilene are going to take our advice and look after your health." Then he added with mock soberness, "They sure must love you, Jim. But you always did have a way with people, I remember."

The marshal had got over his scare. I guess he already saw himself as good as dead, and there wasn't anything to be afraid of after that.

He said, "You'll never get away with it, Pappy. They'll get you. No matter where you go, they'll get you."

"Maybe," Pappy said mildly, "but I doubt it. I hear law dogs don't go snooping around much in No Man's Land, down in the Oklahoma country."

Langly spat. "No Man's Land is a long way off."

I could almost see Pappy grinning in the darkness. I caught a glimpse of steel as he drew his right-hand pistol, and I thought, without any emotion at all, This will be one more to add to Pappy's score.

But he didn't shoot. There was a blue blur in the night, and then a sodden thud as the pistol barrel crashed the marshal's skull. Langly dropped leadenly out of the saddle and hit the ground. Casually, Pappy holstered his .44.

"Now why the hell did you do that?" I said. "You're not going to leave him alive, are you?"

Pappy said, "Jim will do us more good alive than dead. When he gets back to Abilene, maybe he'll send a posse down to No Man's Land. But he'll have a hell of a time finding us there." He looked over to the east. "The Osage country," he said, "down in Indian Territory. That's where we'll make for. The Osages like the cavalry about as well as we do, and white man's law even less." He nodded. "That's the place to make for."

It was a long ride — half the width of Kansas — from Abilene to the northeastern border of the Oklahoma country. But Pappy had traveled it before and he knew every foot of the trail, even at night. We left Langly on the creek bank with a knot on his head and without any pants. Taking the marshal's pants had been something that Pappy had thought of on the spur of the moment, and he still grinned as he thought about it. "Losing his pants," Pappy chuckled, "will be almost as bad on Jim as getting killed. Besides, he won't get back to Abilene in such a hurry if he has to scout around for a horse and another pair of pants."

By this time, doing the impossible, crossing half of Kansas when every law officer in the territory was out to get us, didn't surprise me. I had come to expect the impossible from Pappy. I began to suspect that he would live forever, even with the net drawing tighter and tighter around him all the time, because he knew instinctively what to do at exactly the right time. While Langly, and maybe the army, were cutting tracks all over southeastern Kansas and No Man's Land, we were heading for Indian Territory.

And we made it, in that walk-canter-gallop system of march that Pappy had developed, traveling only at night and going to elaborate pains to cover our trail. We came to the wild-looking hill country, bristling with pine and spruce and hostile Indians — a place where not even the government agents dared to go without miltary escort. And not often then.

We found a natural cave about ten miles from the border, and Pappy said that was good enough. There was plenty of wild game to keep us eating, and water in a small stream for us and the horses.

I remember the day we rode into the place. Pappy stood in the mouth of the cave, grinning pleasantly, not bothered at all at the possibility of having to stay here for months before we dared venture out into civilization again.

"Well, son," he said, "this is going to be our home for a spell. We might as well settle down to getting comfortable."

I felt an emptiness inside me. A kind of hopelessness. I felt as if I had cut away the very last remaining tie to the kind of life I had known before. This was living like an animal, killing instinctively like an animal.

I tried to keep the sickness out of my voice as I said:

"Sure, Pappy. This is our home."

That was spring, in June, and it wasn't so bad at first. We made friends with some of the Osages. They were on our side the minute they learned that we were enemies of the white man's government. Sometimes they would bring us pieces of government issue beef, but not often, because the government didn't give them enough to stay their own hunger. Mostly, Pappy and I lived on rabbits that we trapped, or sometimes shot. Occasionally the Osages would bring us a handful of corn, and we would parch it over a fire and then grind it up and make a kind of coffee. Once in a great while, an Indian would overhear snatches of conversation about the white man's world and would relay the information to us.

It was in August, I remember, when we first heard that Davis was no longer the governor of Texas. But that didn't solve all my problems as cleanly as I had once thought it would.

Pappy said, "Now don't try to rush things, son. It's going to take time to get the army out of Texas, even if Davis isn't governor any longer. And don't forget the Texas Rangers; they'll be taking the army's place. And the United States marshals . . ." Then he looked at me with those sad, sober eyes of his, and I knew the worst was yet to come.

He said slowly, "It won't ever be the same as it was before, son. They won't be forgetting that bluebelly cavalryman you killed, especially the government marshals."

I felt that old familiar sickness in the pit of my stomach.

Pappy said, "Forget about this John's City place, son. You won't ever be able to go back there again. We'll head for the New Mexico country, or maybe Arizona, where nobody knows us." He laughed abruptly. "Who knows, maybe we'll turn out to be honest, hard-working citizens."

But he knew what I was thinking. And he said, "Forget about the girl, too, son. It will be the best for both of you."

I knew Pappy was right. I could look ahead and see how things would be from now on. But I couldn't forget Laurin. She was a part of me that I couldn't put away. Then Pappy's words hit me and I saw a new hope. We'll head for the New Mexico country. Pappy had said. Why couldn't Laurin go with us? If she loved me, if she believed in me, she would do that. I'd change my name and we could homestead a place in New Mexico. We could live like other people there. . . .

Pappy was looking at me with those eyes that seemed to know everything. "Forget about her, son. Women just don't take men like us."

For a moment, I wondered if Pappy was speaking from experience. But that thought soon passed from my mind. The idea of Pappy ever being in love was too ridiculous to consider seriously. Besides, I couldn't forget Laurin any more than I could forget that I had a right arm. She was a part of me. She would always be a part of me.

And I suppose that Pappy saw how it was, and he didn't try to change my mind again.

But he insisted that we stay in our cave until the last of the cattle drives were made in the fall. By then, he said, the army should be out of Texas. If I was bound to go back to John's City, he said, winter would be the best time.

CHAPTER 11

So that was the way it was, because I had learned by this time that it didn't pay to act against Pappy's judgment. We watched August and September crawl by with painful slowness. Then came October with its sudden frosts and red leaves and sharp smells, and I think that was the hardest month of all.

And at last November came and Pappy went out to scout the country to the west, and when he came back he said we could try it, if I was still bound to go. It was a bitter cold night when at last we rode out of the hills and headed south, and we still had on the same clothes that we had worn for months. We were still without slickers, or coats of any kind. But I didn't mind the cold because I was going back to Texas again, to Laurin.

We crossed the Red River far west of Red River Station, on my nineteenth birthday, and Pappy said maybe that was a good sign. Maybe we would make it to John's City and everything would work out after all. But he only said it with his voice, and not with his eyes.

Nineteen years old. I could just as well have been ninety. Or nine hundred. I didn't feel any particular age, in this country where age didn't mean much anyway. Men like Pappy, and Buck Creyton, could have notched their guns long before they were nineteen, if they had been the kind of men to make a show about it.

I was on familiar ground when we crossed the river and got into Texas again. I half expected Pappy to leave me there and go his own way toward New Mexico, but he only said, "We've been together now for a pretty good spell. I guess I wouldn't rest good without knowing how you made out."

It didn't occur to me to wonder what I was going to do or say when the time came to face Laurin. I didn't know how I was going to explain away the reputation I'd got as a gunman, and it didn't worry me until we had come all the way and sighted the Bannerman ranch house in the distance.

And Pappy said, "Well, son, from here on in, I guess it's up to you."

Pappy knew what he was, the things he

stood for. And he knew that he wouldn't do my cause any good if Laurin saw us together. And, for the first time, I saw Pappy as Laurin would have seen him — a hard, dirty old man with ratty gray hair hanging almost to his shoulders. A man in pitiful rags and tired to death of running, but not knowing what else to do. A man with no pride and no strength except in his guns.

Laurin would see only death in those pale gray eyes of Pappy's, missing the shy kindness that I knew was there, too. Laurin would look at Pappy and see me as I would be in a few more years.

I said, "Is this good-by, Pappy?"

He smiled faintly. "Maybe, son. Or maybe I'll see you again. You never know."

I said reluctantly, and Pappy could see the reluctance in my eyes and it made me ashamed, "You might as well come with me, Pappy. The Bannermans set a good table, and we both could use some grub."

But he shook his head. "You go on, son." We shook hands very briefly. "And good luck with that girl of yours." He jerked his big black around abruptly, and without a good-by, without a wave of his hand or a backward look, he rode back to the north.

I watched him until he disappeared behind a rise in the land, and I felt alone, and unsure, and a little afraid. Doubt began to gnaw at my insides.

Good-by, Pappy. . . . Good luck.

I nudged Red gently and began riding over the flatland that I knew so well, toward the ranch house. Toward Laurin. As I got closer the uneasiness inside me got worse. For the first time in months, I was conscious of the way I looked — my own ragged clothes, my own shaggy hair hanging almost to my shoulders. And in contrast, my shining, well-cared-for pistols, tied down at my thighs. No pride and no strength except in his guns. That was the thought I had used in my mind to describe Pappy . . . and all along I had been describing myself.

For a moment, I was tempted to turn and ride as hard as I could until I caught Pappy. Pappy was my kind. We understood each other. . . . But the thought went away. Clothes didn't make a gentleman. Long hair didn't make a killer. Laurin would understand that.

The thought of turning back went away, but not the feeling of uneasiness, as I got closer to the ranch house. I came in the back way, around by the barns and corrals, and a couple of punchers in the shoeing corral looked up and watched for a moment, and then went on about their work. They didn't even recognize me. More than likely they pegged me for a saddle tramp looking for a few days' work, and, knowing that Joe Bannerman never hired saddle tramps, lost interest.

Then, as I rode on through the ranch back yard, I saw a man come out of a barn with a saddle thrown over his shoulder, heading for a smaller corral near the house where the colts were kept for breaking. He glanced at me once without slowing his walk. Suddenly he stopped, looking at me. He waited until I pulled up alongside him, and then he said:

"My God, Tall!"

The man was Laurin's brother, Joe Bannerman. He looked at me as if he wasn't entirely sure that his eyes weren't playing tricks on him. He looked at Red, who had been a glossy, well-cared-for show horse the last time he saw him, but whose coat was now shaggy and scarred in a thousand places where thorns and brush had raked his royal hide.

I tried to keep my voice light, but I knew that the change in me was even more shocking than the change in Red. I said. "How are you, Joe? I guess you might say the prodigal has returned."

But Joe Bannerman had no smile of welcome. He shifted the saddle down to the crook of his arm. "Tall, you're crazy! What do you mean, coming back to John's City like this?"

But he knew before I had time to answer. Laurin. Something happened to his face. He said, "Look, Tall, if you know what's good for you, you'll get out of here in a hurry. There's nothing in John's City for you any more." Then he added, "Nothing at all."

"Don't you think that's up for somebody else to decide, Joe?"

"She's already decided," Joe Bannerman said roughly. "Next week she's getting married."

I stiffened. At first the words had no meaning, and then I thought: Joe never liked me. This is just his way of trying to get rid of me. I even managed a smile when I said, "I guess I won't put much stock in that, Joe, until I hear Laurin say it herself."

He glanced once at the house and then jerked his head toward the barn that he had come out of. "For God's sake, Tall, be sensible. Get that red horse in the barn before somebody sees you."

There was something in his voice that made me rein Red over. I followed him, not quite knowing why, as he walked quickly to the other side of the barn, where the house was blocked from view. I dropped down from the saddle and said, "Now maybe you'll tell me what this is all about."

Joe Bannerman dropped his saddle to the ground and seemed to search for the right words. He said, "I don't want you to get the idea that I'm doing this for your benefit, because I don't give a good round damn what happens to you. But I don't want any trouble around here if I can help it." Then his voice got almost gentle. And I didn't understand that. "You ought to realize better than anybody else," he went on, "that things have changed since . . . since you went away from John's City. You're a hunted man, Tall, with a price on your head."

I said, "You wouldn't be having any ideas about that reward money, would you, Joe?"

"Don't be a damned fool!" he said angrily. "I just want to keep you from getting killed on my doorstep. Like I told you, there's nothing here for you. Why don't you just ride off and let us alone?"

"I'd still like to hear it from Laurin," I said, "before I do any riding." I started to turn toward the house again, but an urgency in Joe Bannerman's voice cut off the movement.

"Goddammit, Tall, listen to me! I'm trying to tell you that it's all over between you and Laurin." Then he sighed wearily. "I guess you've got a lot of catching up to do. I'll try to give it to you as straight as I know how. Ray Novak's in that house, and he has orders from the federal government to get you. Ray was made a deputy United States marshal after the bluebellies were pulled out of Texas. I told you that things changed. . . ."

I think I knew what was coming next. I tried to brace myself for it, but it didn't do any good when Joe Bannerman said, "It's Ray Novak that Laurin is in love with, Tall. Not you. She's afraid of you. You've got to be just a name on wanted posters, like this Pappy Garret that you've been riding with. You've got to be a killer, just like him." He shook his head. "I don't know, maybe you had a right to kill that policeman on account of your father. But all those others . . . What is it, Tall, a disease of some kind? Can't you ever turn your back on a fight? Don't you know any way to settle an argument except with guns?"

Then he looked at me for what seemed a long time. "I guess you don't even know what I'm talking about," he said. "That's the way you always were, never turning your back on a fight. And you never lost one before, did you, Tall? But you're losing one now. It's Ray Novak that Laurin's going to marry. Not you."

I stood dumbly for a moment before the anger started to work inside me. I still didn't believe the part about Laurin. A thing like ours couldn't just end like that. But Ray Novak — at the very beginning of the trouble it had been Ray Novak, and now at the end it was the same way. I started for the house again, but Joe Bannerman stepped in my path.

"Tall, you can't go in there. Ray has been sworn in to get you."

I said tightly, "Get out of my way."

He didn't move.

I said, "This is my problem and I'll settle it my own way. If you try to stop me, Joe, I'll kill you."

His face paled. Then I thought I saw that look in his eyes that I had seen once before — just before he told me that Pa was dead. For some reason that I didn't understand, he was feeling sorry for me, and I hated him for it.

Slowly, he stepped back out of my way. He said quietly, "I believe you would. Killing me wouldn't mean any more to you than stepping on an ant. It wouldn't mean a thing to you."

"Don't be a damned fool," I said. But he had already stepped back, watching me with that curious mixture of awe and fear that I had come to expect from men like him. He didn't try to stop me as I went around the side of the barn and headed for the back steps of the house. Maybe he didn't feel it was necessary, because it was too late to stop anything now. Ray Novak was waiting for me at the back door.

If he had made the slightest move I would have killed him right there. I realized that I had never really hated anybody but him. It would have been a pleasure to kill him, and I knew I could do it, no matter how much training his pa had given him with guns. But he didn't make a move. He didn't give me the excuse, and I'd never killed a man yet who hadn't made the first move.

He said mildly, "I guess you better come in, Tall."

He was just a blurred figure behind the screen door and I couldn't see what his eyes were saying. Then another figure appeared behind him. It was Laurin.

Woodenly, I went up the steps, opened the screen door, and stepped into the kitchen. Laurin was standing rigidly behind Ray, and I thought: She's grown older, the same as I have. Those large eyes of hers were no longer the eyes of a girl, but of a woman who had known worry and trouble and — at last I placed it — fear. She had changed in her own way almost as much as I had changed. Only Ray Novak seemed the same.

Ray said, "We don't want any trouble, Tall. Not here. Maybe it's best that you came back this way and we can get things settled once and for all."

Laurin said nothing. She didn't move. She looked at me as if she had never seen me before, and in my mind I heard Joe Bannerman saying: There's nothing for you here in John's City. Nothing at all. But I fought back the sickness inside me. Laurin had loved me once, that was all that mattered. She still loved me. Nothing could change that.

Ray Novak moved his head toward the parlor. "Do you want to come in here, Tall? We've got a lot to say and not much time to say it in. My pa is coming in from town in a few minutes to pick me up in the buckboard. We'll have to get everything settled before then."

I said, "I can settle with you later. This is just between me and Laurin."

I looked at her and still she didn't move. I couldn't tell what she was thinking. At last she said, "It's Ray's affair as much as ours, Tall. You see, we're going to be married."

I guess a part of me must have died then. Joe Bannerman had said it and I hadn't believed it. Now it was Laurin herself, telling me as soberly as she knew how that it was all over between us, and I knew that this time it was the truth. I wasn't sure what I felt, or what I wanted to do about it. I suppose I wanted to go to her, to take hold of her with my hands and shake some sense into her. Or hold her close and make her see that it wasn't over with us, that it never would be. But her eyes stopped me. Perhaps she had expected something like that, and I saw that look of fear come out and look at me. She started backing away. She was afraid of me.

Ray Novak said, "I wanted you to know about me and Laurin before I went out looking for you. I didn't want you to think that I was going around behind your back. . . ."

I shoved him aside with the flat of my hand and took Laurin's arm before she could back away. She tried to twist out of my grasp, but I held on and jerked her toward me. Anger like I've never known before was swelling my throat. I said, "Tell him to get out of here! If he doesn't, so help me God, I'll kill him where he stands!"

Ray Novak started to step forward. Instinctively, his hand started to move toward his gun, and I was praying that he would follow through with the motion. But Laurin said:

"Ray!"

And he stopped. Then something strange happened to Laurin. A moment before her eyes were bright and shiny with fear, but now they showed nothing.

She said, "Ray, do as he says."

Ray Novak's face darkened. "I'm not leaving you alone with him. He's crazy. There's something wrong and mixed up and rotten in that head of his."

"Ray, please!"

He hesitated for another moment. Then he relaxed. "All right, Laurin. Whatever you say. But I'll be outside if . . ."

He left the rest unsaid. He turned and went out the back door, taking up a position a few paces away from the back steps.

I heard myself laugh abruptly. "So that's the man you're going to marry! A man with a yellow streak up his back that shows all the way through his shirt!"

But I stopped. That wasn't what I wanted to say at all. Anyway, I knew that Ray Novak wasn't yellow. He might be a lot of things, but a coward wasn't one of them.

Laurin said, "Tall, please. You're hurting me."

I turned loose her arm. My thoughts were all mixed up in my mind and I couldn't get the words arranged to tell her what I wanted to say. I found myself standing there dumbly, rubbing my face with my hands and wondering how I was going to explain it to her. If I could only explain it in a way she could understand, then everything would be all right again. But she didn't give me a chance to get my thoughts arranged.

She said flatly, "Why don't you go away, Tall? Go far away so that we'll never see you or hear from you again. Ray will give you that chance, because he knows what you meant to me once. He has been sworn in as a special deputy to get you. He's working for the government, Tall, a United States marshal — but he'll give you a chance if you'll only take it."

I said, "I don't need any favors from Ray Novak!" But that wasn't what I wanted to say, either. "Laurin, Laurin, what's wrong? What have they said . . . what have they done to turn you against me like this?"

She shook her head, a bewildered look in her eyes. "You actually believe that your trouble is caused by other people, don't you?"

Think? I *knew* there wouldn't have been any trouble if it hadn't been for the Creytons, and Thorntons, and Hagans, and Novaks. But how could I explain that to her? Women didn't understand things like that. I remembered what my ma had said, long ago, about my fight with Criss Bagley: But, Tall, why didn't you run?

I said quickly, "Laurin, listen to me. This isn't the end of us. It's only the beginning. It won't be the same as we planned, but we can make it good. We can be together." I took her arm, gently this time, and she didn't try to pull away. "They'll never catch me," I said. "The army, Ray Novak, nobody else. We'll go away. Pappy knows a place in New Mexico. We can go there. We'll be together, that's the only thing that counts. You don't mean it about marrying Ray Novak, it's just because you've heard wrong things about me. You love me, not him."

The words came rushing out in senseless confusion, and they stopped as abruptly as they had begun. The look of bewilderment went out of Laurin's eyes, and amazement took its place.

"Love you?" she said strangely. "I don't even know you. I don't suppose I ever knew you. Not really, the way you get to know people and understand them, and be a part of them. You're . . ." She shook her head helplessly. "You're nobody I ever saw before. You're some wild animal driven crazy — by the smell of blood."

Her voice was suddenly and painfully gentle, cutting worse than curses. She dropped her head.

"I'm sorry I said that, Tall."

But she meant it. She didn't try to get out of that. I turned loose of her and walked woodenly to the door. I pushed the door open, went down the steps and into the yard.

Ray Novak said, "Tall."

I went on toward the barn where I had left Red. I don't know where I thought I was going from there. To catch up with Pappy, maybe, and try to make it to New Mexico with him. Maybe I wasn't going anywhere. It didn't make any difference.

Ray Novak caught up with me as I was about to climb back into the saddle. "I'd better tell you the way things are," he said. "I'm giving you a day's start to get out of John's City country. Then I'll be coming after you, Tall."

I said flatly, "Don't be a goddamned fool all your life. I don't want any favors from you. I'm right here. Take me now if you think you can."

He shook his head. "That's the way Laurin wants it." He hesitated for a moment, then added, "Don't underrate me, Tall. I've learned things about guns and gunmen since you saw me last. I won't be as easy as Hagan, and Paul Creyton, and some of the others. Don't think that I will, Tall."

"You and your goddamned two bullets in a tin can," I said. "You don't even know what shooting is. But I'll teach you. You come after me and I'll teach you good, Ray."

I got up to the saddle and rode south, without looking back. Without thinking, or wanting to think. I didn't know where I was going and I didn't care. I just knew that I had to get away and I had to keep from thinking about Laurin. I should have hated her, I suppose. But I couldn't. And I suppose I should have killed Ray Novak while I had the chance, but, somehow, I couldn't do that either. Not with Laurin looking. I felt a hundred years old. As old as Pappy Garret, and as tired. But, like Pappy, I had to keep running.

I didn't see the buckboard until it was too late. And by that time, I didn't care one way or another. It was old Martin Novak coming up the wagon road from Garner's Store, and I vaguely remembered Ray saying that his pa was coming by the Bannermans' to pick him up. I had forgotten all the rules that Pappy had gone to so much trouble to teach me. I let him get within fifty yards of me before I even noticed him, and by that time things had boiled down to where there was only one way out.

It's the same thing all over again, I thought dumbly. But they never understand that.

Nobody could understand it, unless maybe it was Pappy, or others like him. The monotonous regularity with which it happened would almost have been funny, if it hadn't been so deadly serious. It was like dreaming the same bad dream over and over again until it no longer frightened you or surprised you — you merely braced yourself as well as you could, because you knew what was going to happen next.

Martin Novak had the buckboard pulled across the road. I could just see the top of his head and the rifle he had pointed at me, as he stood on the other side, using the hack for a breastwork.

"Just keep your hands away from your pistols, Tall," he called, "and ride this way, slow and easy."

I didn't have a chance against the rifle,

not at that range. But I felt a strange calm. I never doubted what would happen next. I didn't even wonder how it would end this time, because this time I knew.

But I played it straight, the way Pappy would have done. I said, "What's this all about? What's that rifle for, anyway?"

"I think you know, Tall," he called. "Now just do as I say. Ride in slow and easy, and keep your hands away from your guns."

I nudged Red forward, keeping my hands on the saddle horn. If it had been Pappy, he would have been wearing his pistols for a saddle draw, high up on the waist, with the butts forward. I had forgotten to make the switch, but even that didn't bother me now. I looked at Martin Novak and thought: There's only one way, I guess, to teach men like you to leave us alone.

When I got within about twenty yards of the buckboard, he motioned me to stop. He was wondering how he was going to disarm me, and probably remembering stories he had heard about what had happened to Bass Hagan.

He said, "I don't want to have to kill you, Tall, but I will if you don't do exactly as I say. Now just reach with one hand, where I can see, and unbuckle your cartridge belts."

I said, "Just a minute, Mr. Novak. Hell, I

never did anything to you."

He raised up from behind the buckboard and I could see the star pinned to his vest. The Novaks and their goddamned tin stars, I thought.

"It's more than that, Tall," he said solemnly. "You're wanted by the law. It's my job to arrest you, and that's what I intend to do." He studied my hands, which still hadn't moved toward my belt buckles. But he still had that rifle aimed at the center of my chest, and he wasn't too worried.

He said, "You've . . . been to the Bannermans', I guess."

I said, "Yes. I've been there."

He nodded soberly. "Ray shouldn't of done it," he said thoughtfully, almost to himself. "He should of took you in himself. But," he added, "I guess Laurin wanted you to have one more chance."

I said, "I guess she did." I didn't particularly want to kill him. I didn't have anything against him except that he insisted on making my business his business. And if I killed him I knew I wouldn't get that day's start that Ray Novak had promised. But that didn't bother me. Ray Novak could come after me any time he felt like it. I was ready for him.

For a moment, I thought I'd try to talk

the old man out of it, but I knew that it wouldn't do any good. Like Pappy, I had grown tired to trying to talk to people in a language that they didn't understand. It was easier to let my guns speak for me.

"There's no use holding off, Tall," the old man said soberly. "Just go on and drop your guns."

I looked for a brief moment behind my shoulder. I could still see the Bannerman ranch house. A shot would be heard there, if I was forced to shoot. Maybe they were even watching us. It was possible that Ray Novak was already getting a horse saddled to come after us and try to stop it.

I didn't care one way or another. I had stopped caring about anything when Laurin cut herself away from me. What was there to care about?

I said, "All right, Mr. Novak. I guess you win."

I could see relief in his eyes as I began to unbuckle my left-hand gun. He was slightly surprised and, because of my reputation, maybe a little disappointed because I gave up so easy. But he was relieved. And the relieved are apt to be careless.

I unslung the cartridge belt, but instead of dropping it, I handed it down to him. Instinctively, he reached for it, pulling his rifle out of line.

Marshal Martin Novak was a smart man. He caught his mistake almost immediately. But by that time it was already too late. He was off balance, in no good position to use either pistol or rifle. He knew that he was going to die before I ever made a move toward my other .44. I saw death in those dark, solemn little eyes of his. I thought, You've got all the time in the world. Take your time and do a good job of it. And then I shot him.

The bullet went in just above his shirt pocket on the left side, and he slammed back against the buckboard. The team scampered nervously for a moment, but I pulled Red over in front of them and quieted them down. Martin Novak went to his knees, held himself up for an instant with his hands, then fell with his face in the dust. He didn't move after that.

I sat there for a moment looking at him. Red was nervous and wanted to pitch, but I reined him down roughly with a heavy hand. I heard myself saying:

"I didn't want to kill you, Mr. Novak, but, goddamn you, why couldn't you let me alone?"

Then I realized that he couldn't hear me. And I knew that before long somebody would start wondering about that pistol shot. I pulled Red around and headed toward the hills.

CHAPTER 12

Instinct, I suppose, made me head for the place that had given me protection before, Daggert's Road. It was a fool thing to do probably, because that would be the first place Ray Novak would look for me, but I couldn't think of anything else. I raked Red's ribs cruelly with the rowels of my spurs, even though he was already running as fast as he could.

I looked back once and saw little feathers of dust rising up around the Bannerman ranch yard, and I knew that would be Ray Novak and some ranch hands pulling out to see what the shooting was about. Well, they would find out soon enough, but by that time I would be in the hills. . . .

Suddenly, all thoughts jarred out of me. The world became a whirling, crazy thing, and I crashed to the ground and the wind went out of me. For a moment I lay stunned, gasping for breath. I shook my head, trying to clear it. After a while I tried moving my arms and legs. They were all right. I just had the breath knocked out of me. Finally, I pulled myself to my knees and looked around. And then I saw Red.

He lay quietly behind me, looking at me with big liquid eyes, full of hurt. "Red, boy! What's the matter?"

I dragged myself to my feet and limped over to him. His right foreleg was twisted under him. His blood was staining the ground, and I glimpsed the awful whiteness of bone that had broken through the hide. Then I saw what had happened. Because of that crazy run I had forced him to over this rough ground, he hadn't been able to judge the distance correctly. He had been thrown off balance at a small gully jump that ordinarily he would have taken in stride. His leg had snapped as he went down.

For that moment I didn't wonder how I was going to get away from the posse that was sure to be coming. I knelt beside Red, taking his head in my arms and rubbing my hands along his satiny neck and shoulders. "It's all right, boy. Everything's going to be all right." But those hurt eyes knew I was lying. I loved that horse more than I loved most people. Red was all I had left. And now I didn't even have him.

I think I would have cried — sitting there on the ground, holding Red's head in my lap — like some small child who had broken its best-loved toy in a moment of anger, not realizing what the loss would mean until it was too late. But then I looked down on the flatland and I could see Ray Novak and the others ganged around the buckboard. They were the ones responsible, I thought bitterly. Not me.

I stood up slowly, anger making a red haze of everything. I could see them wheeling now, not much more than specks in the distance, and heading in my direction. I thought, Let them come! It all started with Ray Novak — let it end with him. I was ready to meet him where I stood. I was *eager.*

Then a voice said: "You'd better come along, son. There's not much time."

I wasn't particularly surprised. I had come to expect the impossible of Pappy. I turned and looked up the slope, and there he was, sitting that big black of his, mildly rolling one of those corn-shuck cigarettes. He nudged his horse gently and rode on down to where I was, seeming entirely unconcerned with the posse charging across the flatland toward us. He glanced once at Red, and then looked away.

"I'm sorry, son," he said gently. "He was a good horse."

"Pappy, for God's sake, what are you doing here?"

He shrugged slightly. "It's a long trail to travel by yourself."

It was the closest thing to sentiment, or regret, or fear, that I had ever heard in Pappy's voice. From the very first, I figured that Pappy had picked me up because he needed a kind of personal bodyguard, but I knew now that it wasn't that. It had never occurred to me before that a man like Pappy could be lonesome. That he needed friends like other people.

I said, "Pappy, get out of here! Go on to New Mexico, or wherever you were going. You can't help me now."

But he only smiled that sad half-smile of his. Then he shook a boot out of a stirrup and held it out. "Just step up here," he said. "I guess this black horse won't mind riding double for a little piece."

"Pappy, you're crazy. You can't expect to outrun a posse by riding double."

He shrugged again. "But we can find a better place than this to fight from. Come on, son. There isn't much time."

Pappy's word was law. I knew that he wouldn't budge until I did as he said.

Dumbly, I put my foot in the stirrup and swung up behind him.

I glanced at the posse. They were already in rifle range, but they were holding their fire until they had us cold. Then I looked at Red, knowing what I had to do, but not knowing if I had the guts for it.

"Just look away, son," Pappy said softly.

There was one pistol shot, and Red lay still.

Good-by, Red. Good-by to the last thing I ever gave a damn about, except Pappy. And I wasn't even sure that I cared a damn about Pappy. Maybe he was just something to hold to, a device that men like us used in order to live a little while longer. I felt empty and angry and there wasn't much sense to anything.

The big black took us as far as the top of the ridge, and that was the end of the line. We could hear the hoofs pounding now as Ray Novak pushed his posse of ranch hands on up into the hills after us. The black was a good horse — as good as Red, maybe — but he couldn't carry two men and be expected to outrun the sturdy range horses chasing us. When we hit the crest of the rise Pappy dumped out of the saddle, clawing that fancy rifle of his out of the saddle boot. I came off after him and the black went on down to the bottom of the slope.

"Over here, son!" Pappy yelled. And when I stopped rolling I saw that he already had a private fortress picked out for us. Three big rocks gave us cover on three sides and we could sweep the hill with fire in all directions. As I crawled up beside him, Pappy already had that rifle in action. He fired twice and two of the posse dumped out of their saddles and lay still. That cut the original five down to three, and I thought maybe we would get out of this after all, if we could catch one of the loose horses, and get rid of Ray Novak.

But Novak and the two ranch hands began to scatter before Pappy could cut any more of them down. They scrambled for rocks near the base of the hill and for a few moments it was quiet. Those two dead riders gave them something to think about before trying anything foolish.

Pappy looked at me, grinning slightly. "Well," he said, "we've been in worse places. That's always some consolation, they say."

I said nothing. I searched the land below us, but nobody was moving. It was quiet — deadly quiet. I wondered what Ray Novak was thinking down there. The Novaks and their tin badges! After looking at his pa, he would know that tin badges didn't make a man immune from bullets.

Pappy stacked his rifle against the rock, got out his makings, and began to roll a cigarette. Like a man knocking off work for a few minutes to take a breather. There was no way of knowing what he was thinking. For a moment he stared flatly down the side of the slope; then he looked at me.

"It didn't work out, did it, son?" he said. "I didn't think it would, but I was hoping. . . ."

I knew he was talking about Laurin. And I didn't want to talk about Laurin. I didn't want to think about her.

Nodding his head toward the bottom of the hill, he said, "He got her, didn't he?" meaning Ray Novak. "I think maybe I knew from the first that he would. It was just a feeling, I guess, after you told me how things were."

"Cut it off, will you, Pappy?" I said angrily.

"Sure, son, I didn't mean to butt in." He sat back against the rock, with that cigarette dangling between his lips. "He's a good man, though," he said thoughtfully. "He damn near put a bullet in me that day. Probably he's learned some things since then. I don't think I'd be in any hurry to stand up to him now."

"He's a goddamned tin soldier riding

behind a tin badge," I said. "His pa was the same, but he died just as easy as anybody else."

Pappy's eyes widened. "You killed his old man?"

"Sure I did. He tried to arrest me."

Pappy shook his head sadly from side to side. "Maybe we're going to have trouble," he said heavily. "Maybe we're going to have more trouble than we ever saw before."

It was still quiet down on the slope. I said, "This is no good. We can't run, and we can't fight if they don't come out from behind those rocks. But we can't just sit here. By now, somebody from the ranch will be headed toward John's City for more help. We've got to get away from here before that comes."

Pappy nodded and spat out his cigarette. Then a horse nickered back behind us and I could almost see Pappy's ears prick up. "Just a minute," he said. "I'd better look after that black of mine."

He crawled on his hands and knees to the naked side of the hill and peered down below. Suddenly, something jabbed me in the back of the brain. Intuition, they call it. Or hunch. Some men have it and some don't. Sometimes, when it hits you, it tells you to put your stack on the red and all you have to do is watch the roulette ball drop in. Or it may tell you that around the next corner is sudden death. When I felt it, I whirled and yelled:

"Pappy, look out!"

But the moment had passed. It had come and gone and I hadn't got my bet down in time. I heard a rifle crack in the afternoon, and I turned just in time to see Pappy go down.

"Pappy!" I yelled again.

But I knew it was too late. I ran over to where he was, silhouetting myself against the sky, but not caring now. Then I saw the rifleman — that sober, stone-cold face that was past anger, or grief, or any emotion at all. It was Ray Novak.

I didn't stop to wonder how he had slipped around to the naked side of the hill. He had done it, and that was enough. Dumbly, he was looking at me now. Probably, he had figured it out cold and clear in his mind what he was going to do to me when he caught me, but suddenly finding himself face to face with me startled him. And that was Ray Novak's mistake. I shot before he could swing the rifle around.

I watched as the bullet slammed into his shoulder, jerking him around. He went to his knees and began tumbling down the side of the hill.

Instinct told me that he wasn't dead. There was only a bullet in his shoulder and that wouldn't stop him for long. But before I could do anything about it, the two ranch hands were drawn around to the naked side of the hill by the shooting. I aimed very carefully at one of them. I could see horror in his eyes as he started backing away, too scared to use the gun in his hand. I pulled the trigger and he fell away somewhere out of my line of vision. I forgot about him.

I didn't bother about the other posse member. Like a damned fool, he forgot that I was in perfect position to kill him and went running across the open ground to where Ray Novak was stretched out unconscious. For a moment I watched as he pulled Novak out of the line of fire and I thought: Let him go, there's no use killing him. I knew he would get Ray back to the ranch house as soon as he could, and that would take care of the last of the posse. And, anyway, there had been so much killing, maybe I had lost the stomach for it. Then I remembered Pappy.

He was crumpled at my feet as limp and lifeless as a discarded bundle of dirty clothing. I turned him over gently and straightened his long legs. "Pappy!"

But he didn't move. And a sick feeling inside told me that Pappy wasn't going to move. The bullet had gone right through the middle, about three inches above his belt buckle, but there was only a little blood staining his dirty blue shirt. All the bleeding, I knew, would be on the inside. I felt his throat for a pulse and it was so faint that I imagined that it wasn't there at all. After a moment the glassiness that was beginning to crowd his eyes receded just a little, and that was my only way of knowing that he wasn't dead.

I didn't know what to do. There was nothing I *could* do, except to stay there beside him and not let him die all alone, the way he had lived. I didn't even have a drink of water to give him. I couldn't think of anything to say that might make it any easier. Down at the base of the hill, I could hear a horse scampering and I knew that would be the ranch hand taking Ray Novak back to the ranch house. Soon it was quiet again, except for the dirgelike mourning of the wind and the rattle of dry grass.

I knelt there watching the glassiness returning to Pappy's eyes. Vaguely, I wondered what his last thoughts were, if there were any thoughts. I wondered if I was a part of them. Was there any sorrow, or

273

regret, or dismay at the way he had used his life? Would he use it any differently if he had the chance to live it all over again?

I got my answer when, for just an instant, his eyes cleared. He looked at me, smiling that sad half-smile. Then he spoke quietly, precisely, as if he had thought the matter over for a long time.

"You were right, son. I should have killed him that day . . . when I had the chance."

So that was the way Pappy died — with no dismay and only one regret — sorry only that he had made the mistake of leaving a man alive. I stood up slowly, looking up at the endless sky. I think maybe I wanted to pray for Pappy — but what was there to say? Who was there to listen?

Good-by, Pappy. That was all I could think of. The wind moaned, cutting through my thin clothing, and I realized that winter had at last come to Texas. Winter was the time for dying. I bent down and closed Pappy's staring eyes. Sleep, Pappy. You can rest now, for there will be no more running for you. And Pappy's quiet face said that he was not sorry.

I left Pappy there on the hilltop with the wind and the sound of the grass. I took his rifle and went down to the bottom of the slope and found his big black horse trembling like a whipped kid down in the bottom of a gully. I said, "Easy, boy," and stroked his sleek neck until he quieted down, and then I swung up to the saddle.

I headed west again, higher into the hills, and not looking back at the hill where Pappy lay. Pappy was gone. Nothing could be done about that. First my pa, then Laurin, and now Pappy. I had lost them all, as surely as if they were all dead, and in the back of my mind one name kept burning my brain. Ray Novak.

I didn't bother to cover my tracks. I purposely left a trail that a blind pilgrim could have followed, because I knew that before long Ray Novak would be coming after me. It would be only a matter of hours before he got his shoulder patched up, and I knew him well enough to know that he wouldn't allow a posse to track me down. He would do it himself. That was the kind of man he was. And that was the way I wanted it — just me and Ray Novak.

I found the place I wanted, a ragged bluff overlooking the lowland trail that I had been following, but I traveled on past it for a mile or more and then circled around to approach the bluff from the rear.

It was perfect for what I wanted to use it

for. I could see all approaches to the bluff, and anybody passing along the trail I had taken would have to come within easy rifle range. That was the important thing. All I had to do was wait.

And think.

I tried to keep my mind blank except for the job I had to do, but I couldn't keep the thoughts dammed up any longer. I couldn't go on shutting Laurin out of my mind and pretending that she never existed. She had existed, but she didn't any more. Not for me. I had lost her, and where she had once been there was only emptiness and bitterness. I had to admit it sometime, and it might as well be now.

The hours were lonesome dragging things up there on the bluff, and the wind was cold. The wind died as night came on, but the chill was worse and I didn't dare risk a fire. There was nothing to do but wait.

The night became bitter cold, and a frost-white moon came out and looked down upon the bluff. That night I learned what it was to be alone. And I learned something else — that fear grows in lonely places. I hadn't let myself think about it before, but now I began to wonder why I had chosen this way to take out my hate on Ray Novak. Why didn't I wait for him on the trail and face it out with him, the way I had done with Buck Creyton?

The night and the moon, I suppose, had the answer. I was alone. And nobody really gave a damn whether I lived, but a great many people were wishing me dead. There was no comfort in anything except perhaps the feel of my guns, but that wasn't much help. I could hear Pappy saying: Maybe we're going to have more trouble than we ever saw before. Pappy was dead, and Ray Novak was still alive. He damned near put a bullet in me that day, Pappy had said, and probably he's learned some things since then.

Then Ray himself saying: I won't be easy, Tall. . . .

I was scared. Worse than that, I was scared and I wouldn't admit it.

Somehow the long night wore itself out, and dawn came at last, cold and gray in the east. I got through the night without running, and that was something. I wondered how many more nights there would be like that one, and cold sweat broke out on the back of my neck.

But with the daylight it was better. The sun warmed me, and Pappy's rifle had a comforting feel in my hands again. And, instinctively, I knew that I wouldn't have much longer to wait.

But it was almost noon when I finally saw him. He came riding out of the south, along the trail I had left for him, and suddenly I realized that it would be so easy that I was amazed at the worrying I had done the night before. The distance, I judged, was about two hundred yards — not close, but plenty close enough if you had a rifle like Pappy's. I took a practice aim, judging the distance and the wind, and adjusted the leaf sight on the rifle.

I won't be easy, Tall, he'd said. Well, we'd see about that.

I waited until he reached the top of the grade before I brought him into the sights again. And then I had him, the center of his chest framed in the V of the rear sight, the knob of the front sight resting on the bottom of his left shirt pocket. It was a beautiful thing, this rifle of Pappy's. Once I had thought that a man would almost be glad to get killed by a gun like that, if he had any kind of love for firearms. I wondered how Ray Novak would feel about that.

I drew my breath in until my lungs had all they would take. Then I held it. The sights were still on the target. All I had to do was squeeze the trigger.

But I waited. A few seconds one way or

the other wouldn't make any difference. I studied the man in my gunsights, the man who had all the things that could have been mine. Security, respect, and most important of all, Laurin. If it hadn't been for Ray Novak, all of them could have been mine. Now was the time to pull the trigger.

But I didn't. Sudden anger caused the rifle to waver, and I had to let my breath out and go through the whole thing all over again.

Laurin . . . I could have had her, if it hadn't been for him. Maybe I could still have her, with Novak out of the way for good. But that thought went out of my mind before it had time to form. She had showed clearly enough what she felt for me — fear, and maybe a kind of pity. I didn't want that.

For a moment, while the sights were settling again, I wondered what Laurin would do, what she would say, when they brought Ray Novak's body in with a bullet through his heart. I wondered if being hated was worse than being feared.

I told myself to stop thinking. Squeeze the trigger, that was all I had to do. But my finger didn't move. I had never thought of it that way before. It was little enough, but at least she didn't hate me. Not yet.

And she wasn't alone. That was important

now, because I was beginning to learn what it was to be alone. And I guess that was when I began to understand that I wouldn't pull the trigger to kill Ray Novak. Somehow, in killing him it would be like killing a part of Laurin. . . .

I snapped the leaf sight down on the rifle. I'm sorry, Pappy. I guess my guts are gone.

And up on that hilltop with the moaning wind and rattling grass, I imagined that Pappy smiled that sad smile of his.

I watched Ray Novak until he was out of range, out of sight, and I wondered emptily if he would keep looking for me until he finally found me. As long as he was a United States marshal he would keep looking. I knew that. The hurt and the hate would burn themselves out in time, but not that sense of duty that the Novaks prided themselves on.

Then I had a sudden, strange feeling that, somewhere, Laurin wasn't fearing me any more. Nor hating me. It occurred to me that a man didn't have to stay a United States marshal — especially if his wife was against it.

But there was little comfort in the thought. If it wasn't Novak, there would always be others. The army, the sheriffs, the bounty hunters. Or punk kids wanting to make reputations for themselves.

I thought of Pappy then, not with sorrow, but with a feeling near to envy. I went over to that big black horse of his and stroked his neck for a moment before climbing on. I holstered the rifle, checked my pistols, and then we headed west.